RED ONE

Rod J Bergeron

RED ONE

Rod Bergeron
3360 Harwood Road, R.R.#1
Baltimore, Ontario, K0K1C0
Canada

Edited by Elizabeth Dickson

ISBN 0-9734232-2-6

PART 1
The Heat of the Day

I look down at my hands. My palms are sweaty; I wipe them on my pants. I glance down the row of seats at my people. Gord Johns sits beside me, he is my point man and first aid specialist. Beside him is Terry Sims, my best shot and also an explosives expert. Beside Sims sits Chris Caloway. Caloway is the rear guard and also the communications expert. I look across the plane at the British Colonel and give him a smile, he smiles back. Further back I see the Load Master talking on his mike. The light above him turns from red to yellow. He taps his fists together. I know that means we have a communications link. I press the black button on my chest and I hear chatter in my ear piece. It's the pilot talking with the AWACS Commander. AWACS is short for Airborne Warning and Control System. The AWACS plane flies high overhead. I hear the AWACS Commander ask for our call signs and confirmation of our communications link. I am third after the two British Officers and two American Officers after me. All together there are five teams of four: two British teams, two American teams and one Canadian team.

After the two British Officers give their call signs and confirmation of their communications links it is my turn. I say, "Call sign Red Leader, comms link confirmed." I know if we are doing our comms link we must be getting close. We are probably somewhere over the Indian Ocean, past Saudi Arabia and probably turning south. It's 2340 hours and I know we jump sometime around 2400 hours, so we have about twenty minutes left. I go over the pre-jump checklist in my mind one more time. Weapons checks were done on the ground so were harnesses and chutes. I see everyone has their bag between their feet and their helmets on their bags. Going over this checklist just makes me more nervous, I stop.

It's a long trip down from 38000 feet. It will take us over four hours to get down and cover the 200 kilometres to Somalia. The Load Master gives us a wave with his hands that tells us to get up. We all slip our arms into our harness, stand, put on our helmets and fasten ourselves. The Load Master comes around and gives each of us a once over. He taps us on the helmet to give us the all OK. He goes back to his place and fastens his harness to the wall.

It's two minutes to drop. I reach down and point to my face mask and oxygen canister. Everyone takes their masks and puts them on. I turn the small red knob and the oxygen starts to flow. There is this terrible grinding in the floor of the plane. I realize the rear door is opening. I face my team and they face the rear of the plane and see the door opening. We all grab each other by the shoulder harness. The wind rushes through the plane like a hurricane. The Load Master holds up one finger to tell us one minute to jump. My heart skips a beat. I take a deep breath and wait. The lights go out, I lower my night vision gear onto my face and I turn it on. Everyone else does the same. I take another deep breath and release it slowly. The light beside me goes green. I run backwards as my guys run forward; three steps and we are out. The night is black. Our night vision gear turns the night into neon green. I am still holding onto my guys shoulders as we rush away from the plane. Then I feel a hand on my ankle, it's one of the other team's linking up with us for the fall. I feel another hand on my other ankle. My ear piece crackles under the noise of the wind and then I hear the AWACS Commander, "All teams are linked." They can see us using infrared cameras. He tells us it's 15 seconds to break. It feels like an hour. We have a long way to go. We hear the break command and we all let go at the same time. I count to five and pull my cord. My chute opens. I am jerked to a quick stop. My equipment bag dangles below me and sways back and forth.

I look up to check my chute. It is fine. I reach up and grab my two toggles to steer. I look around and I see my three guys are right beside me. They all give me the thumbs up sign. It's almost too easy this time. I wait to hear the AWACS Commander because at night we can't see shit. The only way down is to have someone tell us where to go. I have a small compass and an altimeter on my wrist. I look down to see what direction we are going. We are heading north which is the direction I thought we should be going in. The AWACS Commander breaks the long silence. He tells us we are at 34000 feet and to continue heading north. I set myself heading north and my guys all line up beside me.

I look to my right and see the two British teams; the two American teams are on my left. I look at the British

Officers and they give me a thumb up and I return the same. Then I look at the two American Officers and give them a thumb up and they give me the same. I start to breathe again. The two British Officers do a radio check with their guys and I do the same. "Red leader to red team, radio check over." They each take a turn replying. "Red two, comms ok." "Red three, comms ok." "Red four, comms ok." Usually these guys would be fucking around by now but since we have company they are all on their best behaviour. Thank Christ. Now the Americans do their radio check. Everyone is very professional tonight.

My crotch starts to hurt a little from the harness. I try to adjust it but it only makes it worse. I flex my leg muscles and then slowly release the muscle to try and relax them. It works. I look back at my compass to see we are still heading north towards Somalia. I try to bring a little levity to the situation, "Hey does anyone else have really bad bag nag?" Everyone gives a little laugh. I think even the British Colonel may have cracked a smile.

Ah the Brits. Never has a country turned out so many tight asses. I swear if you shoved a chunk of coal up their ass in two weeks you'd have a diamond. You have to respect their straight forwardness though. They really tell it like it is. If you're an asshole they will tell you so to your face. These guys are serious and professional and they all still really seem like a good bunch of guys.

My mind starts to wander a little. I think of my wife and three kids back in Baltimore Ontario. I wonder if they are sleeping right now or outside playing in the warm July sun. Maybe they are out by our pool giving their mother hell about something. I really miss them. I wonder if they are thinking of me or where I am. I hope they are not. I don't need them worrying about me and what I'm up to.

Johns always asks, "I wonder if the people of Canada ever think of us when they are in their warm safe beds at night?" I bet the answer is, "Not a fuckin' chance." We always have some deep debate over why they should even care about us at all. Who the fuck knows? I know all of our families care about us. That's all I really care about.

Once again the AWACS Commander breaks the silence. "AWACS command to all call signs, you are on course at

31000 feet and 22 minutes AWACS command out." I immediately think to myself, "Holy fuck we are only 22 minutes into a four hour drop." I look down into the darkness. I see nothing below us. The night vision gear makes everything look a florescent green. I never really found them hard to get use to, but I know Johns really has a hate on for them.

I look over at my guys and catch their eye. They all look back at me. I pull my left toggle a little and then my right. I do this a couple of times to get my body swinging side to side. As soon as I start, my three guys all do the same. We have done this before just as a way to pass the time. It must have looked like fun because right away the Americans all started to do the same. The Brits held fast, no one moved until the British Colonel said, "What are you waiting for boys have some fun." He was the first to start. So here are 20 highly trained, highly experienced soldiers fucking around at 31000 feet above the Indian Ocean. We do this for a couple of minutes and we all laugh. We all stop and get back to business.

My legs are going to sleep a little so I keep flexing my leg muscles trying to keep some blood moving through them. We are staying aloft for so long because we need the AWACS plane to guide us into Mogadishu. We were to do a HALO jump (high altitude low opening), but we collectively decided that it would be best to do a long descent in so we could make full use the AWACS. I think I may be regretting this now.

I look down at my altimeter on my arm once again. We are at 29000 feet. I can't see the time; I don't want to know. I want to chat with the others around me but we are to maintain minimal radio contact. We don't want anyone to know we are coming. I go over the plans once again in my head. We are to land in a small clearing just past a wooded area near the end of the runway. After we get all of our shit together we are to make our way to the terminal and tower and secure them with as little confrontation as possible. We hold until the first helicopters and planes can get there to relive us. Sounds good in theory but seldom does a plan go off without a hitch. I just remind myself that these guys all know their shit. We were all handpicked for this mission and everyone here volunteered to do this.

Rod Bergeron

This was not going to turn out the way it did in 1993. This time we were coming to win. This time we had NATO at our backs and we were the first 20 men of a 20000 man task force coming to put this little shit hole back together. This time we are to eliminate the warlords, not negotiate with them. We are to free the people and turn this boot camp for terrorists back into a free and safe society, whether they liked it or not. The world had had enough of the Bin Laden network in the early 2000's. The world had learned that you cannot in fact negotiate with terrorist. They don't play by the same rules or any rules for that matter. The West had long known that the Somalia government had been taken over by terrorists if not overtly, then covertly. They were not kidding anyone. When these assholes blew up the United Nations building in New York with a dirty nuclear bomb everyone knew it was Hasad in Somalia. Everyone! He had promised this a year ago. This time we didn't have to play nice. This time we are coming hard and fast.

The silence is once again broken by the AWACS Commander. "AWACS command to all call signs, you are at 27000 feet and 82 minutes. You will need to change course. Ease right. We will monitor." We all ease to the right slightly. We then wait to see if there are any further commands. The AWACS Commander comes back, "AWACS command to all call signs, hold your current course, we will advise AWACS command out." I think to myself, "One and a half hours we are not doing too bad." The feeling is back in my legs but I have to continually work at it. I don't want to hit the ground with legs that are fully asleep. I don't think it would be wise to hit the ground with legs that don't work. I look at my oxygen canister. It reads half full. I think we will have more than enough. I look around to see everyone. They all look kind of bored to tell the truth. They are barely close enough to see but they look as bored as me. My mind starts to wander again. I start to think about my family back at home again and I stop myself. I have to stay focused on the mission.

I look down and I can see through the clouds a little. I point down and look around to see whose eye I can catch. To my surprise everyone is already looking down. Through the darkness you can see some coast line and a few scattered lights here and there. We can see how far we have left to go and really it is not that far. I look at my altimeter again and we are at 22000 feet. It looks like our last course adjustment has put us right on track. Everyone is looking down now and pointing to different things. We are like a bunch of kids trying to get their parents attention. I can see lights a long way off. It is really a beautiful sight. Like little fireflies across the night sky. At least now we have something to occupy our minds. We can see the western coast of Africa now. The clouds are beginning to part. I start to get a little inpatient and really just want to get on with this mission. Every minute we get closer to our target I remind myself not to rush this, I know we have to take it slow and everything will turn out fine.

The AWACS Commander corrects our course a couple or more times over the course of the next hour until we are a couple of kilometres away from the LZ (Landing Zone). Before we go into the site the AWACS does a heat signature search of the area; he tells us that there are no persons near or around the LZ. I know he will update us before we move to the hangers and the tower.

We all spread out and let the first American team land. They quickly land and get clear of the LZ. They pick up their chutes and gear and move out. I signal my guys to get more distance between us and to get some altitude. We are too low and we have a couple of minutes until it is our turn. The second American team moves in and they clear their equipment. They are actually faster than the first group. Everyone on the ground moves very quickly. I can see some of them already have their weapons out and are setting up a perimeter.

Now it is our turn to land. I go in first and land hard. My legs feel like they weigh a thousand pounds each. The rest of my guys are on the ground very quickly. I grab my chute under my right arm and my bag and start to get out of the way. I can't stand so I drag myself on my hands and knees. My guys are right behind me. I drag my chute over to where the Americans are and shove it under a small tree. I open my equipment bag and pull out my assault rifle. I find the silencer and fasten it on. I load my magazine and cock the weapon. I look to see my guys already done. I usually beat them but not tonight. I check my watch its 0352.

Rod Bergeron

My fucking legs are killing me. I get out of my harness and stick it under the tree. I try to get my legs moving a little but they are really stiffening up. I don't have a choice, they have to move. One of the American Captains sees I'm having a problem and he comes quickly over to me, "Cramped up?" he asks in a very low voice. "Yes and they are killing me," I reply. "You need a drink of water," he suggests. I grab the tube to my camelback and take a long drink. He does the same. Now my guys have seen me and hurry over. "Fuck don't tell me you broke your leg," Johns says quietly. "No just really bad cramps," I quickly retort. "You need a drink," he says like my mother would. I take another drink.

I swing my hand in a circle above my head, they all know that means to make an all round defence. They move quickly into a large circle. By now everyone is on the ground and we have hidden all of the chutes. We have all of the equipment out and are just taking a quick breather.

The other officers come over to where I am to discuss our next move. The British Colonel asks me if I'm alright. I assure him it is just a cramp and it is getting better every minute. It is starting to feel better. I can actually feel something now. I speak up first, "Do we want to do food and water now?" Everyone agrees. "I have to take a piss," the one American Officer states. "OK let's go to fifty percent and do food, water and toilet," the British Colonel says in a very low whisper. He then broadcasts it to all of the other men over our intercom. "Fifty percent," means half of us are going to maintain the perimeter while the other half eats, drinks and pees.

I am finally close enough to the Colonel to see his name tag, it says, "Morton." I think I forgot his name the second he said it. This guy is a Colonel for a reason. He is a natural leader, he's full of confidence I would say he is around fifty years old, but just as fit as the rest of us. He speaks with a firm yet even tone and he generally only speaks when he has something to say. His hair is hidden under his helmet and everything is still green from the night vision gear but I can still tell his hair is cut very short and just as grey as mine. I don't know if our hair is grey from age or from doing this job for so long. His clothes fit him like they were tailored and there is not a thread out of place. His face doesn't have a drop of fat on it. If I had to describe him in one word it would be, "Tough."

I can see all the men divide up. Half keep their positions on the perimeter and the other half sit, eat and drink or find a tree to pee behind. No one makes a sound. I take another drink from my camelback. My legs are starting to lose the pins and needles feeling. I move my legs slowly and can feel the muscles coming back to life. Johns comes over to me once again. "How's the legs?" he asks. "Getting better," I reply, "Help me up for fuck sakes," and he grabs my arm and stands me up against a spindly tree. My legs are starting to feel much better. I take a couple of steps and then kneel down on one knee.

I grab an energy bar from my right front pouch on my web gear. I open it and eat it quickly. I move silently back over to where my bag was left and search for my extra bottle of water. I find it and think, "This is piss warm." I take a mouthful and then another. I take off my camelback and pour the rest of the bottle into it. I look around to see everyone is finishing eating and drinking and I see Johns go over to relieve Sims. Everyone took a turn and I didn't have to say a word. Wow, they really are on their best behaviour today.

All of us officers move back into the centre just as we get a call from the AWACS Commander. "AWACS Commander to all call signs," he calls. Colonel Morton being the senior most officer answers back. "Leaders are converged AWACS Command send over," he says calmly and quietly. The AWACS Commander replies, "AWACS Command to all call signs the area to the east to the main terminal is clear of human heat signatures, begin movement on your time." Which to us means, "Quit fucking around and get moving." We look at each other like we have just been spanked and each move back over to assemble our teams.

My legs are much better now and really starting to loosen up. It is our turn to take the lead. I look at my guys and they know it's time to go. I hold up my right hand and move it from front to back in a straight line a couple of times and they know that means we are going in single file. I move out from the cover of the trees to a deep ditch on the north side of the road. The ditch has a very sandy

Rod Bergeron

bottom with thin, foot- long, prickly grasses on both sides and the odd rock mixed in with the sand. The ditch is a good height to hide in being almost a metre deep. The road is mostly sand as we are only a couple of hundred metres away from the ocean, the air smells of the sea. The temperature is very warm even for the middle of the night. A sliver of a moon hangs over the ocean.

We move along the ditch about two hundred metres and I stop, holding up my right fist for all to see. I look back to see that everyone is now out of the trees. No one makes a sound. I call for the AWACS Commander, "Red Leader to AWACS Command." The AWACS Commander replies, "AWACS Command, send message over." "Red Leader we are in place to begin our assault, any unfriendlies? Over," I ask. "AWACS Command, there are two persons in the terminal northwest corner, persons are together. We will monitor them while you move, over. "Red Leader, we are moving, signal if we need to stop, over," I say as we start to move. "AWACS Command, we are monitoring, out," he assures us.

I raise my weapon's eye piece up to my night vision gear

for the first time this mission. I look ahead just to reassure myself. I raise my hand and give the signal to move ahead. Once again I am in the lead. "Red Leader to all call signs, let's keep this fast and tight," I command. I hear back from all the leaders in sequence, they all agree. I am crouched down and moving very quickly along the ditch. There is about five meters between each of us. No one dares to break pace. We cover the kilometre to the terminal in about five minutes. I raise my fist for all to see and bring everyone to a halt again. I look back, everyone stops instantly.

The tower is about twenty metres high and attached to the terminal. It is made of ordinary concrete blocks and painted yellow. The top is painted a bright red colour. The tower has large three metre high windows on all four sides with small screened windows at the bottom of each window. There is a single door at the bottom of the tower that is the only entryway. The terminal is a bright yellow colour with lots of windows and doors on the front and back. The terminal is filled with benches and seats and has three separate counters to purchase tickets. The two hangers are right beside the terminal and each one has large front doors that face the runway. The hangers are made of metal and have rounded sides and flat roofs and are large enough to hold two or more small commuter jets. There is a chain link fence gate that separates the terminal from the hangers.

I check back with AWACS Command. "Red Leader to AWACS Command, what's the position of those hostiles over," I ask. I wait what seems to be a very long minute. I look down the row of men and I see each one of them is scanning the area looking for any sign of movement. "AWACS Command to Red Leader, hostiles are in same local, northwest corner on the terminal," he states clearly. "Red Leader out," I reply. I point my three fingers at my three guys and point to the tower. They move in that direction very quickly and silently. Everyone is about three metres apart. I am the last to go. I go around to the far side of the tower and find the door leading upstairs, it's unlocked. I point to two of my guys, Johns and Sims, then I point to the stairs; they move up them silently and quickly, Johns leads the way, he is the point man. I am the last one up the stairs. Caloway stays at the bottom to guard the door way. I check my watch, it's 0423.

"Red Leader to all call signs, the tower is secure," I announce. I take a deep breath for the first time since we landed. I know we are only part way through but this is a big part. We need this airport if we are to get the heavy equipment in. "AWACS Command, understand that Red Leader, other call signs are clear to begin, hostiles still in northwest corner of the terminal," is his reply. "Green Leader, I understand ball is mine," states Colonel Morton. The British Colonel is to move in and take the two men in the terminal with the least amount of noise possible and by any means. If at all possible the two men will just be captured. We don't know if they are armed or just some night watchmen. If they don't have to shoot they won't.

Sims quickly unpacks his sniper rifle, loads and is set up. He pushes out a screen and takes up his position. Johns takes a position looking down the runway, I take a position looking out towards the ocean and Sims takes a position looking towards the road where any incoming traffic would come from. "Red Leader to Red team, all clear," I state. My guys all report back in order, "Red two clear, Red three clear, Red four clear." I close the conversation, "Red Leader, all clear, out".

Sims is a very quiet guy. He is tall and very athletic, the kind of guy you would think of as a runner. Like most snipers that I have met he is somewhat of a loner, but when you need someone to count on he is your guy. He is a really good listener and has eyes like a hawk. He is able to pick out movement with the naked eye that I can't see with binoculars. To say Sims is a good shot is like saying the Mona Lisa is a nice little painting.

Time seems to stand still. It seems like forever and we have not heard a sound from anyone in ten minutes. I take that as a good sign, the least noise the better. I stare out over the land and ocean in front of me. It is eerily quiet. I turn my mike off and look over at my two guys, Johns and Sims. "You guys OK?" I query. "I'm holding out, how about you LT?" questioned Sims. "I'm good, how about you Johns?" I enquire. "I'm fine, I guess no news is good news, eh", Johns suggest. "I'm going to run down and check Caloway, I'm turning my mike back on," I tell the guys. I turn and walk silently down the steps. Near the bottom I see Caloway peeking out the door. I turn my mike off again. "Caloway, how you making out?" I ask. "Good LT, how about you?" he replies. "I'm good, you

need anything?" I question. "I could eat a fuckin' horse"
he says. "We'll get you some food as soon as we get this
shit hole locked down," I say. I give him a thumb up and
head back up the stairs. I turn my mike back on.

Johns reaches up and covers his mike, "How's Caloway?"
I cover my mike, "He's good, hungry but good." "That
fucking guy could eat all day, the skinny little bastard,"
says Sims. I'm just about to say "Cover your fucking
mike," when Caloway chimes in. "That's what your wife
says too," he jokes. There it is. For the first time since we
left someone is making a wife or mother joke, there goes
the best behaviour.

Caloway is our joker, a really funny guy with a heart of
gold. You would never meet a kinder more caring person,
which makes me wonder why the fuck he's here.
Caloway had a really troubled childhood. His father was a
violent drunk that beat him, his brothers and sisters as well
as their mother. One day Caloway woke up and his
mother and two sisters were gone. Caloway and his
brothers went to school and told their teachers what had
happened and they ended up in a foster home. That's all I

know of the story. He told us this one night when he was pissed out of shape and has never spoke of it again. Anyway my wife and I have kind of adopted Caloway as our own grown son. He eats dinner with us most nights and just hangs out a lot of the time.

We wait for what seems like ever and still nothing. There is not a sound anywhere. And then it comes.

Colonel Morton speaks up, "Green Leader and Blue Leader to AWACS Command, Hostiles captured and confined, Terminal secure." "AWACS Command, understood, Orange and White teams go for securing hangers," he says quickly. That is the cue for the Americans to secure the hangers. Once again there is nothing. Long silences make me nervous. Two minutes later we hear from the Americans. "Orange Leader to AWACS Command, Orange and White teams have the hangers secure," he states.

"AWACS Command to all call signs, great work guys. Both air support and ocean landing craft are approaching your area soon," promises the commander. We know that just off shore there are Marines in landing craft waiting to get into action. There are also helicopters on the way from their aircraft carriers to land at the airport. All we have to do is wait for them to get here and our job is done. It is 0511 and the sun will be coming up soon. We don't want to be alone when the sun comes up.

Hasad controls everything that happens in this country. Hasad has more than a small army. He controls more than 2000 men and he is very well equipped. The Chinese have been selling him weapons for 12 years. Hasad has been selling the Chinese some of the world's best diamonds in exchange. Our twenty man force will be no match for 2000 heavily armed terrorists.

It is time for the next phase of the plan. I call to the leaders, "Red Leader to Green, Blue Orange and White Leaders," I pause, waiting for their attention. They reply quickly, "Green Leader send over, Blue Leader send over, Orange Leader send over, White Leader send over," they all confirm. "Red Leader to all call signs, deploy your snipers," I ask. "Green Leader copy that, Blue Leader copy that, Orange Leader copy that, White Leader copy

Rod Bergeron

that," they all confirm.

I cover my mike, "Sims go." He moves to a small ladder bolted to the wall at the top of the stairwell. He climbs up to make it onto the roof of the tower. The other snipers are now making their way onto the roofs of whatever buildings are available. Snipers usually get to pick their own spots; they just know what direction they are to cover. We now have four snipers on the rooftops.

"AWACS Command to all call signs, helos and landing craft making their way to your position now, AWACS Command out," he states clearly. The next thing I can hear is the sound of the helicopters coming towards us. I look out towards the ocean. I can't yet see the landing crafts or the helicopters. This causes me great concern. If I can hear the helicopters so can everyone else.

"AWACS Command to all call signs, there are two pickup trucks with multiple hostiles about two kilometres north or your position and closing fast, weapons are free, we will continue to monitor," he gives us a bleak warning. My heart skips a beat. This is where the shit starts to happen.

I think clearly, this is where I excel. "Red Leader to Red Team, Johns to the roof, Caloway lock the door and move up the stairs to the first landing, weapons are free," I say clearly and assertively. "Weapons free" is a sign to all persons that they can fire their weapons as needed.

I go over to the wall where the ladder is and call up to Johns, "Spank 'em, take these." I throw two hand grenades up to him. "Will do," is his reply. I turn back to the windows and look north. It's starting to get light out now, I take my night vision gear off and slide it into my left front pouch and snap it shut. My eyes adjust quickly to not seeing green anymore. It takes a couple of seconds and then my eyes are fine.

I go over to one of the small windows at the bottom of the large tower window, open it and push out the screen. I look north and just as I do I hear the distinctive fire of a sniper rifle, then four or five more shots in quick succession. Now I can see the two grey pickup trucks with fifty caliber machine guns mounted in the back moving quickly towards us. There are seven or eight men in each pickup truck. The lead pickup truck is moving wildly all over the road as it approaches us. Then there is multiple sniper rifle shots and both trucks go wildly into the ditch, one on each side of the road about two hundred meters from us.

In the far off distance I hear the Scorpion helicopters more clearly now, I know they are getting close. Then I hear the sound of a fifty caliber machine gun, and then there is more and more machine gunfire. It's not the guys in the pickup trucks, none of them seem to be moving. I believe the snipers got all of them. I quickly turn to the south window and look towards the ocean. Now I can see the landing crafts as they are getting closer to the shore. Finally, some reinforcements are within reach. Now we have to make sure these guys can make it onto the beach safely.

Just as I see the landing crafts AWACS Command calls to us. "AWACS Command to all call signs, multiple hostiles moving towards your location from the east and west. Hostiles on foot and truck," he quickly warns. AWACS Command no sooner says this than there are multiple sniper rifle shots ringing out. In the distance once again there is fifty caliber machine gunfire. I feel the wall of the tower hit hard repeatedly and I know that there is a large machine gun firing at us with some accuracy. I look west down the runway to see a pickup truck moving very quickly towards us and firing a lot of rounds and then another burst hits the tower walls.

I stay down low and look towards the west. I move over to the small windows open them, and push out all the screens. The Scorpion helicopters are really close now. I hear the helicopters fire many rounds but I can't see them, so they must be on the east side of the building. Right in front of my position is another pickup truck coming down the run way. I raise my rifle and aim directly at the driver and fire two rounds. The pickup truck moves wildly to the right and then back to the left, two men fall out of the back. One man gets up right away and raises his rifle at me in the tower. I fire two more times hitting him directly in the chest; he falls to the ground lifeless. Flurries of shots ring out from the snipers above me and the rest of the men from the pickup truck fall to the ground. The Scorpion helicopters are right on top of us now and are firing rounds at the tree lines and are advancing out towards the areas where all of the men and pickup trucks have been coming from. A fierce battle breaks out in front of us, the noise deafening; the air is heavy with an acrid smell.

The AWACS Commander is once again in my ear, "AWACS Command to ground units, that pickup truck has to be moved off the runway can you assist?" I am the closest, "AWACS Command, Red Leader, I will attempt to move it." I race down the stairs and see Caloway. "Stay put cover me," I order him. He nods back at me. "AWACS Command to all ground units, cover Red Leader he is out of the building to move the pickup truck on the west side of the runway," he strongly says. I crouch down with both hands on my riffle. I sprint towards the pickup truck about two hundred metres from me. I cover the distance in about thirty seconds. As I make my way there I see some of the men on the ground still moving. None look in good enough shape to shoot me so I continue. The air is full of smoke and the smell of gun powder, the sun is beginning to heat up the tarmac. The tarmac around the dead and dying is covered with blood and broken pieces of automobile glass.

I get to the driver's side of the pickup truck and open the door. I grab the dead driver who is slumped over the steering wheel and throw him out onto the ground. As soon as his foot comes off the brake pedal the pickup truck starts to move forward. "It's still running," I say to no one. I catch up and jump in. I pull the pickup truck off the runway, drive towards the tower, throw it in park and jump out running. Caloway is right in front of me as I run towards him. "LT your fuckin' crazy", he says with a laugh. "AWACS Command, good job Red Leader," he says pleased.

"AWACS Command to Scorpion Leaders, you may begin your landings," the AWACS Commander says to the Scorpion helicopter pilots. Within seconds the first helicopters are on the ground and the men are running towards the tower and the terminal.

Caloway opens the door and directs the first team up the stairs. The first team is a group of airmen who are air traffic controllers. "Thank Christ you're here," I say to them with a smile. They smile back and get right to work setting up their own equipment. They have large black boxes with all types of equipment in them. They have practiced this before in only a couple of seconds they are set up and calling AWACS Command.

I look out the tower window and see more and more helicopters land and take off over and over again. I look towards the ocean and see the second and third waves of the landing crafts drop men and equipment off over and over again. It is a beautiful sight. I think to myself, "Fuck we are lucky." I feel relieved if only for a second. Just then the AWACS Commander is in my ear again. "AWACS Command to Red team, Green team, Blue team, Orange team and White team, regroup in terminal for further orders," he insists. I look up the ladder to see my guys coming down already. "I thought we were done," Sims says to me as he walks by. "We're never fuckin' done," I say back. It is now 0628.

We hustle over to the terminal and meet up with everyone else. No one seems worse for the wear. Everyone gathers in the centre of the terminal which is really just a large room with a bunch of chairs and benches for people to sit. I grab a drink from my camelback and everyone else does the same. I open my front webbing pocket and pull out an energy bar and wolf it back quickly. I look around to see most are doing the same. One of the Americans goes over to the vending machine and smashes the front glass on it and grabs an OH Henry. Several others go over and grab a bunch of candy and bring some over for the rest of us. Everyone eats something. I feel like a kid standing around with friends on the schoolyard at recess.

Then the AWACS Commander breaks in, "AWACS Commander to Red team, Green team, Blue team, White team and Orange team, a helicopter with an assault team has been shot down 27 kilometres north of your present position, that team was en route to take control of Hasad's diamond mines. We need you to take two Scorpion helicopters to that position and rescue the survivors. There are six survivors. Then take control of the diamond mine, by force if necessary. Are there any question from the leaders?" "Red Leader, is there any backup?" I ask. "AWACS Commander to Red Leader, as assets are freed up they will be made available to you," he states. "Blue Leader to AWACS Commander what is the primary mission?" he requests. "AWACS Commander to Blue

Leader, as always primary is the survivors. The mines are within eight hundred metres of the survivors, leave a medical team with the survivors place them on your Scorpions and take the mines with force if required," he emphasises. "AWACS Commander to all teams, any further questions?" he asks. "White Leader, what type of helio was it?", he asks. "AWACS Command, GN32 heavy lift," the AWACS Commander answers. We all look at each other. "AWACS Commander to all teams, if no further questions the two Scorpions outside are yours, resupply of food, water and ammo is on board AWACS Command will monitor, AWACS Commander out," he finishes.

Everyone gets their things together and we quickly head out to the tarmac. The first pilot waves us in. Our team, the Blue team and half of the Green team head to the closest Scorpion; the others hurry over to the other Scorpion and everyone climbs in. I go in the side door and everyone follows me in, I move to the back. I grab a bottle of water out of a case on the floor as I move past it. I find a seat and do up my seat belt; I hold the water bottle and realize it is cold. I take my helmet off and rub the cold bottle across my brow several times. All I can think of is how great that feels. I open the bottle up and slowly let the cold water pour down my parched throat. Never has a drink felt so good. Someone slides a cardboard box down towards me. It's full of energy bars. I think to myself "Man cannot live on energy bars alone." I pass on them.

The Scorpion helicopter is one of the most advanced weapons systems ever created. It is fully integrated with all of the state of the art electronics of the AWACS. It can receive telemetry from many different sources: ground troops, satellites, drones and AWACS. One of the reasons why the infantry love it, is its ability to provide information to troops before they actually hit the ground. There are ten electronic pads on the ceiling that can provide each troop with instant real time information. We call them TUFF Pads. I grab the pad which is on an extension spring and pull it towards me. I enter my service number and touch the map button at the top right. Johns leans over towards me to take a look. I am instantly looking at our current location and I can see our helicopter and the terrain we are over. I touch the map with my finger and drag it towards the downed helicopter and switch views to heat signature. I can see there are six heat signatures still moving and several that are not. I have learned that just because someone is not moving does not mean they are dead.

Then again I touch the screen with my index finger and move towards the diamond mine. There are lots of heat signatures from people. It would seem that most of them are moving but not in an aggressive way. They seem to be working. There are a couple of heat signatures with weapons. They do not seem to be concerned about the downed helicopter or maybe they just can't hear it or see it yet. The guys across from me grab their own pads and start to look at the information, some are looking at maps some are looking at the poor bastards that were shot down. The Scorpion helicopter is now moving very quickly as I look out the small window everything is a blur.

I push the pad's spring back up to the roof, I look down at my weapon and take the magazine out and refill it with the ammunition at my feet. I take out my empty magazines and fill them with fresh ammunition. I put the magazines back into my pouches on the front of my web gear. I look down the row of guys, give them a little wink and cock my weapon. I put my helmet back on and finish my water. I lower my goggles from the top of my helmet onto my face. I instinctively know there will be a lot of sand flying about as we land.

"AWACS Command to all call signs, two minutes to landing, there are no hostiles in your area, stabilize any injured, the Scorpions will be nearby when you are ready for extraction, AWACS Command out," he says confidently. Colonel Morton gets everyone's attention and makes a large circle with his hand above his head. That is the sign for an all round defence. Then he speaks so that the people in the other Scorpion can hear him, "Blue Leader to all call signs, set up an all round defence, all medical persons to the wounded, make stable and prepare for evacuation, Blue Leader out." Everyone knows what their job will be when they hit the ground. I see a couple of people grab the larger medical bags from the overhead storage and a couple of others unfasten the stretchers form their overhead storage. We are ready to go.

"AWACS Command to all call signs, LZ one minute out," he warns. LZ is the landing zone. When we land, all three doors will open, both sides and the rear. I am closest to the rear door. I hear and feel the engines beginning to slow; I know we are going to land in a second. All three doors open at once we are still ten metres off the ground. The hot air rushes in and we continue lower. At two metres the lights go green and we start out. I jump clear, land on my feet and move towards the downed Scorpion helicopter. I turn to look at everyone else getting out and they are all now clear of the Scorpion.

I hear a couple of shots and ricochets; I quickly turn back to see that someone is shooting at our Scorpion. The rounds continue to hit it hard and fast. I hit the ground. I am now the person furthest from the LZ. I call to the AWACS Commander, "Red Leader to AWACS Command, Scorpions are taking heavy fire, where are those rounds coming from?" "AWACS Command to Red Leader wait out." He wants me to wait. Everyone is on the ground now. I look around, there is no high ground anywhere near us. The gunfire must be coming from the ground somewhere. My team crawls up to where I am lying. There is a two metre sand dune in front of me. I look right and left, the other teams have moved up along to the same sand dune we are at. I look up to see the two Scorpions are now far off in the distance waiting for us to call them back.

Scorpion helicopters for the most part cannot be shot down by any amount of small arms fire or even large caliber machine gunfire. The Scorpion's body is heavily armoured with Kevlar as well as something called Hard Skin 2. Hard Skin 2 is the densest armour ever created, and the lightest. A one inch thick piece cannot be cut through by anything, it is fire proof and will not rust or decay. These things are tough. The rotor blades of the Scorpion are only half the length of a regular helicopter but twice as wide. The difference makes the Scorpion faster and more manoeuvrable. The Scorpion also has four fifty caliber machine guns and three different types of missiles. The weapons are so vast that the Scorpion requires its own weapons officer. In most helicopters the co-pilot and the pilot are responsible for the weapons.

It seems like a month until the AWACS Commander

comes back on. "AWACS Command to Red Leader, there is a predator drone en route to your location, approximate time of arrival sixty seconds, wait out," he commands. I hear the hum of the drone and know it is close by.

I see the drone fire several small missiles and hear them explode. The AWACS Commander is back on, "AWACS Command to all call signs, predator has destroyed hostiles, way is clear." This is the way we fight in the twenty second century. We rely heavily on eyes in the sky to tell us what is out there and let them destroy the threats; a lot less of us go home in body bags.

I stick my head up and I can see the helicopter, it seems to be torn in two. It is about three hundred metres in front of us. I stand up and start to run; the whole line of men do the same. A perimeter is set up around the biggest chunks of the Scorpion. All of the medical specialists go to see what help they can be. I take my other two guys over to the smaller chunk of helicopter to check it out. It is clear there is no one and nothing inside of it. We race back to the other site. The perimeter is set up and the medical persons are hard at work. They are starting IV fluids on the injured and helping to free a couple of men from the wreckage. I go over and help.

The other leaders are there already. It is a gory sight. I help one of the medical persons push up a large chunk of the seats in order to get one guy's leg free. His leg is bleeding profusely. I grab a pressure bandage quickly and hold it on the large gash on his right inner calf. I sling my riffle behind my back to get it out of the way. I tie the loose ends of the pressure bandage around the back of his leg and pull them around to the front and tie them off tight. I push my hand down hard on the wound. His blood fills the bandage and my hands are quickly covered. I look him in the face and say, "Hang in there." I look at the medic. "How are we doing here guys we got to move?" I ask bluntly. "Almost ready," one of the Americans says who is just finishing with an arm injury. No one else answers. I raise my voice, "How about it guys?" Now everyone answers. They are all ready or almost ready. We get who we can onto stretchers.

There are seven dead in the helicopter or around the area. Not all of the dead are inside of the helicopter. It is more than gory. There are body parts and blood all over the inside and outside of the helicopter. Everything and everyone is covered in blood splatter and little pieces of other people. The pilot, co-pilot and gunner are all obviously dead. They are mostly cut in half by the front console and the floor is driven up into their chest and necks. My hands and arms are covered with blood only seconds after being inside of what is left of the helicopter.

I call it in. "Red Leader to AWACS Command, we are ready for evac." I am more than clear. "AWACS Command to Red Leader, helos in bound now", he states. "Red Leader to all call signs, I'm sending my medical persons out," I am suggesting they all go. "Blue Leader to all call signs, they all go right?" He is looking at everyone else to agree. They all nod in agreement. "Blue Leader to AWACS Command, we are sending all of our medical persons, bring them back ASAP," he suggests. "AWACS Command to all call signs, will return medical persons ASAP, out," he agrees.

It doesn't sound like a big deal sending five guys out of the battle, but when you are only twenty people to begin with it is a significant amount. Any force that is cut by twenty percent has been drastically reduced. I am sure all of us have thought this but none of us have voiced it. We all know that the injured need the medical persons more than we do.

The injured are all on stretchers, except for the three that can walk. The Scorpions are almost on the ground now. We all turn our back to the Scorpions to avoid the sandstorm it creates and we cover the injured with our bodies. We rush the walking over to the closest Scorpion helicopter and a couple of the wounded on stretchers; everyone else goes to the second Scorpion. "We will see you guys back here soon," I scream at Johns. He nods back. He looks at me like he is certain he will be back in the fight soon. The side door shuts automatically and we run back toward the downed helicopter. They are soon out of sight. The whole evacuation and first aid took only eleven minutes. I think to myself, "Fuck we are good."

We now need to move onto the second phase. We have only about eight hundred metres to go but fatigue and the heat is really starting to get to all of us now. It is now

0921. We have all been up for almost twenty four hours and we didn't get much time to sleep the day before. I sit down in the shade of the downed helicopter and take a big drink from my camelback. It is hot now, probably around ninety five degrees. I wipe my head with my glove and then take both gloves off and put them in my right side cargo pant pocket.

I grab my mike and reposition it in front of my mouth. "Red Leader to AWACS Command, send SITREP, over," I request. A SITREP is a situation report. There is a brief pause. I look at the other leaders as if to say, "What the fuck?" I point to the Blue Leader and he instinctively knows I want him to call AWACS. "Blue Leader to AWACS, send SITREP, over," he asks. There is another pause. I am starting to get worried. Then he comes back, "AWACS Command to Red and Blue Leaders, wait out," he pleads. I am thinking that there is something really wrong. There is a lot of action around us. In the distance we can hear helicopters and the odd gunshot. There are a lot of planes overhead. I believe the AWACS Commander is very busy right now. He has been up as long as we have and has been running a lot of different things both for us and everyone else.

"AWACS Command to all ground units, wait out," it's a different voice. They must be changing commanders. What a fucking time to be switching. They probably have some rule about how many hours they can work. I wish we had that rule. But then again we live for this shit. Living this close to the edge of darkness is what we live for. "AWACS Command to all call signs, new leader, SITREP is as follows, heavily armed men still control the mine area, there are no civilians in sight. It is believed they are all in the mine. Heavily armed men control the entrance and three machine gun emplacements surrounding the area. There are no drones currently available for tasking. You must proceed independently. Questions in one minute," he states clearly. We don't have a drone to help us and we are five men down. Shit, this may not be as easy as I thought.

"AWACS Command to all call signs, any questions?" he asks. "Red Leader, no questions, Green Leader no questions, Blue Leader no questions, Orange Leader no questions, White Leader, no questions," we all agree.

"AWACS Command to all call signs we will monitor your progress, AWACS out," he states.

I pick up a chunk of broken metal and hand it to the Blue Leader, Colonel Morton and point to the sand. He nods and takes it from my hand. All five of us leaders are assembled in the shade of the downed helicopter. Colonel Morton being the senior leader should be the one to make the plans about this assault. He has a lot of experience and from what I have seen today he is more than capable. I don't believe anyone here would question any plan he would make, I also believe that if one of these guys didn't like a plan they would most definitely speak up. Everyone here is an independent, strong-willed person.

Colonel Morton reaches for his mike's mute button and turns it off, we all do the same. "I saw on the TUFF Pad on the way in that there are three machine gun emplacements in a triangular configuration around the mine. There are also multiple guards around the mine and its entrance. I believe that we can neutralize the three machine gun emplacements with three teams using their snipers and have the other two teams cover the entrance.

We can wait until everyone is in place and all fire simultaneously. If all are neutralized at the same time we have a better chance of them not calling for reinforcements," Colonel Morton states clearly and authoritatively. "Any questions?" he asks. "Which teams do you want to go where?" I ask. "Since you asked you can take the far emplacement, Orange take the one on the left, White team take the emplacement on the right, Green and Blue teams will take the front and the mine entrance," he clearly orders. "Any more questions?" he asks. There are no questions. "OK we go in 5 minutes, brief your teams, stay in communication, mikes on, let's get this done," he says confidently.

I return to my team of three, myself, Sims and Caloway; Johns is gone back with the wounded from the Scorpion helicopter. I am really going to miss him; he helps keep me grounded. I have left my mike off until I brief my team. "OK here is the news; we are going to take the far emplacement. Sims you are to neutralize all hostiles from a distance. We are going to do this simultaneously so no one is able to call for back up. Any questions?" I ask. They both shake their heads knowingly. "Let's go, mikes on," I order. "Red Leader to Blue Leader, good to go," I state. "Blue Leader to Red Leader, you may begin, let me know when you are in position, Blue Leader out," he states.

I look at my compass. We have to head toward the northwest. I see a line of dunes that should provide us with sufficient cover. I point in that direction. The sand is hot and gritty against my hands. I can feel sand in my boots and around my goggles. I try not to brush it away around my goggles, I know it will only work its way into my eyes if I do. I think about my legs for a minute. They feel fine now; at the LZ they were killing me.

I reach up and turn my mike onto mute. "OK guys we are going around to the far side, absolute noise discipline. I will give further details about the neutralization when we are in position, any questions?" They both shake their heads no. "OK lets go then, Sims you lead; let's use these dunes on our left and head out and then back," I say with confidence. I reach up and turn my mike back on. I call to AWACS Command, "Red Leader to AWACS and all call signs, moving into position now." "AWACS Command to

Red Leader and all other call signs, begin moving into position now. We will monitor, AWACS Command out," he finishes.

I point in the direction of the dunes I want Sims to follow. We move with about three metres in between us. We need to move far out around the position we are going to attack so as not to be seen. The heat coming up from the sand dunes is cooking us; I now know what my Sunday dinner roast feels like. I think about taking a drink from my camelback and remember that is almost dry. I had better save whatever water I have for later. We move slow and low around the six foot high dunes being careful not to be seen. I am in the middle with Sims in the lead and Caloway behind. Sims stops, telling us to do the same with the hand sign of a raised fist. He points to his right and looks to see if we are looking in that direction. I pull out my binoculars and crawl up to where he is; Caloway looks back and around to check behind us. We have only gone about three hundred metres.

When I reach Caloway he points to where he wants me to look. I hold my hot binoculars up and focus them in the direction he is pointing. I can see a position that is only about four hundred metres away. I think we are to close. I point back towards Caloway and we crawl back. I point back towards the direction we just came and I take the lead. I lead us out further into the desert away from the position. I know we have to get out and away in order to not be seen and get set up for the best possible shot. We move west out into the desert for about ten minutes and then head back north to find a new position.

I look down to check my compass and we are heading in a north direction. I think we have gone far enough. I move over to the edge of the dune and hold my binoculars up and scan the horizon to see if I can see the hostiles. They are directly ahead about three hundred metres. I point them out to Sims. He gives me the thumbs up. I call to AWACS Command, "Red Leader to AWACS Command, Red Team in position and setting up now." "AWACS Command to Red Leader, understood wait until remainder are in position. We will monitor." He is waiting for the others.

Sims changes his ammunition and sets up his bipod and

gets ready. The emplacement is directly in front of us. It appears to have two men in the bunker. It is about four metres across and about one metre high. It appears to be made of sand bags all around with a sheet metal top. The desert has pushed sand up around the emplacement as to almost completely hide the fact that it is even there. I can see the two men move around a little and I wonder if they are looking at us. I assume that if they saw us they would be firing already and they aren't. Caloway goes back a little ways to check our rear. He returns to give us the thumbs up. All is clear. The desert sun burns us badly now and we are all low on water. There is nowhere to hide from the heat of the day.

Sims is set up now and I take up a position on his left and a little behind him. I hold my binoculars up and can still see the two shadowy figures. I lay my rifle down beside me and wait. I wish our medical guys were back but we are too far ahead for them to catch up to us now. I worry that if something goes bad here not only are we five men down but we are also missing all of our highly trained medical persons.

Now I hear all of the other Team Leaders confirm that they are in place and setting up. I think to myself, "Thank Christ we're cooking out here." I lay there with the ancient Metallica song "My Friend of Misery" running through my head. I have had this song playing in the background of my mind ever since we took off in Germany. My wife had just given me the MP7 of Metallica before I left. Then I hear all of the other Team Leaders say they are in position and set up and ready to go. AWACS wants to confirm with me, "AWACS Command to Red Leader, confirm your status," he requests. "Red Leader to AWACS Command, we are setup and ready," I say clearly and confidently. "Roger that Red Leader. All teams thirty seconds to go," he warns. I tense up and then try to relax. I see Sims open and close his hands a couple of times and then blinks and looks down his scope through his goggles. He whispers, "I got em." I relax a little. "AWACS Command to all call signs, fifteen seconds on my MARK, ...ten seconds," he once again warns. Time seems to stand still when I am in these types of stressful situations; all you want is for the AWACS Commander to say MARK so we can fire.

Finally, the AWACS Commander says, "MARK." Sims fires his rifle once quickly and then once more right after. I continue to look down my binoculars and see both men hit one after the other. I continue to look and see no further movement. I hit my mute button and look to Sims. "See any movement?" I ask. "Not a fucking thing," he replies. "Let's move up," I say. I hang onto my binoculars in my right hand and my rifle in my left and we crouch down low and move up. There is still three hundred metres between us and the emplacement. We use the dunes to cover our advance towards the emplacement. There is no communication chatter at all. At about two hundred metres we stop to take another look. I crawl to the edge of sand dune and Sims is beside me and Caloway continues to check out rear for any hostiles.

"See anything?" I ask Sims. "No, I smoked those two for sure," he states confidently. We get up onto our knees to move ahead, still crouching. I look back at Caloway still checking our rear for hostiles. He gives me the thumbs up. We continue to move up toward the emplacement and again I stop our advance and peer ahead. At about one hundred and fifty metres we stop again and I look into the emplacement. Now I can see into it very clearly with my binoculars. Sims is beside me. "Nothing," I say with my mute button still off. "I told you," Sims states.

We come around a large dune and are only about seventy five metres away from the emplacement. Sims passes me and is in the lead. I think to myself, "Snipers are grisly little bastards and always want to see how much mess they have made." Then a burst of machine gunfire comes in our direction. I hit the ground fast. Sims is hit and falls hard onto his back. He turns and looks towards me. "FUCK!" he screams. I roll to my right just as another burst is fired. Another round hits Sims. I fire a quick burst and then I hear Caloway fire a couple of quick bursts. "LT!" Sims screams in pain as if begging for help. I figure Caloway is now covering me. He is shooting a lot of rounds towards the emplacement. I get to my feet and grab Sims by his webbing with one hand and start to pull him back. Calloway continues to fire from his position on top of the dune now. I continue to pull Sims until we are behind the safety of the dune.

I am concerned about him, but more mad than anything.

As I look at my friend and comrade a hatred grows inside. Never in all the missions we have done together has anyone of my people ever got so much as a sliver and now I have to worry about the life of someone I am responsible for. Sometimes this fuckin' job sucks.

There is a lot of communications chatter. I remember to hit my mute button to turn my mike back on. "Red Leader to AWACS Command, taking heavy machine gunfire, priority one, one member hit twice, require immediate medical evac, send support," I say very quickly and forcefully. He comes back quickly, "AWACS Command to Red Leader, Understood, Will assist, Medical evac in bound now, all call signs Red Leader needs some help, any extra persons respond now." He's not asking, he's ordering. I hear more chatter as if everyone is answering at the same time.

I turn to Sims to have a look at his wounds. I see a hole in the left side of his shirt and a big hole in his leg and a lot of blood. Nothing is coming out of his mouth, which is a good sign. "Sims, just the leg and chest?" I question him as I tear his shirt open. "Yeah," is all the answer he can give me. His chest wound is a through and through, which means the bullet went right through his chest, on the very outside edge of his chest. "You are one lucky son of a bitch Sims, the bullet went right through. It's hardly even bleeding," I joke with him. "Let's have a look at the leg," I smile at him. I pull my knife out and tear the pant leg open, and see a hole that goes straight through again, only this time it is from left to right. I grab Sims' pressure bandage from his webbing. I apply a lot of pressure to the leg wound and it won't stop bleeding. I call to Calloway. "Caloway get the fuck down here!" I scream to him. He comes quickly. I'm holding the pressure bandage on. "Take his belt off," I plead with him. He undoes his belt and pulls it through the loops. He looks at me "Tourniquet?" he questions. Sims grabs me and says, "No tourniquet, I'm not losing this fucking leg." He knows if there is a tourniquet on his leg chances are it will have to be amputated. I push him down. "Sims I'm going to do everything I can," I assure him. I tie the belt a little loose around his upper thigh. I stick his knife sheath into the hole and turn it tight. "Caloway hold this," I get him to hold the knife sheath. "There it's stopping, it worked," I say to him.

The blood slows to a trickle. Under his leg is a deep puddle of blood and it gets sucked up into the sand. The sand is a dark brown under him. I look at my hands they are covered with his blood. I feel my anger turn to hatred. I don't like the feeling. I pick up my rifle. "Caloway stay here with him, someone is coming to help," I promise them. "Where you goin' LT?" Caloway asks. "I'm going to kill that fuck,", I say with confidence.

I go to the side of the dune and look down my scope. I don't see any movement, but I didn't last time either and Sims got two bullets for it. I decide to go. I look down my rifle sight as I move quickly forward. I sprint a little. I am only about twenty metres away from the emplacement so I cover the distance quickly. I move along the side looking for the entrance. Nothing inside moves. I hear a low moan and then speaking in a language I do not recognize. I move quicker and keep my rifle up at the ready. As I move around to the rear of the emplacement I see an opening going down. There are a couple of stairs made of sand bags. I hear the moaning again. I rush down and in and quickly. I look at the three men inside. The first two on my left are obviously dead, the third is moving towards his hand gun; without a second thought I pull the trigger and hit him directly between the eyes. He falls back dead instantly. "Fucker," I say angrily to no one. My blood still boils with hate.

I don't believe a soldier is to hate. Hate gets in the way. Hate makes you angry and anger clouds your judgement and allows your feelings to get in the way of your job. A soldier shouldn't allow his actions to be clouded by emotion. Everything we do out here could be considered immoral, but out here we will do anything to accomplish our mission. It's what our country asks of us. Immoral yes, but that's the fuckin' job. If my behaviour is to be judged then I will be my judge not someone else that has never been in my shoes, not someone else who has not paid the same price as me.

I race back to Sims and see that there is an American team member already there. "LT, make out OK? I think this leg might just make it," the American says to me. "Yeah I made out OK, I knew this tough bastard would make out alright," I say to the American.

"Tell me you got him LT," Sims says with a smile. "I got him," I smile back at Sims. "You really think the leg is going to be OK?" I ask the American. "I'm no doc, but I don't think it hit the femoral artery. I think it just hit a vein in there somewhere. I'll do my best," he says confidently.

"AWACS Command to Red Leader, send SITREP, over," he asks cautiously. "Red Leader to AWACS Command, one member two major injuries, first aid being assisted by other team member. I request immediate medical evacuation. Our position is secure, hostiles eliminated," I say with some pride. "AWACS Command to all call signs, confirm emplacements secure and guards are eliminated," he is asks for confirmation. All of the other call signs confirm that their positions are secure.

"AWACS Command to all call signs, your medical personnel are returning to you now, load your wounded and regroup, await further orders, AWACS Command out," he clears us. One of the Americans also sustained a leg wound and he is going out with Sims. The Scorpion helicopter lands and the four medical persons jump out, weapons in hand. Sims is lying in a poncho and six of us pick him up, three on each side. I see Johns for the first time in a while. There is a lot of noise from the helicopter, so I have to scream at Johns. "Hey there, you're fuckin' late. Go with Sims he has a chest wound and a leg wound. I'll catch back up with you at the airport," I tell Johns. "Ah shit I missed all the fun," Johns says disappointed. I nod to him, with a little grin on my face.

As they board the Scorpion and fly out of sight, wave after wave of American Marines, and British and Canadian Infantry land in Scorpion helicopters. Within minutes there are hundreds of marines fanning out to secure the diamond mines and free the slaves Hasad had working in there. When we get our first look at these people they look like little rags of humans. Thin frail bodies, rags for clothes, eyes sunk into their skulls, some barely alive. They move like ghosts across the barren landscape not quite sure where to go or what to do. I think to myself, "This is why we came here, now what. What happens to these people, who will help them now?"

We have done all we can do. Now it will be up the people of this little patch of dirt and the governments of the world to put this place back together again.

Rod Bergeron

Epilogue

Sims was flown directly to the Canadian medical ship Life Preserver. Sims had his surgery within an hour after he left us and was flown to Germany for further surgery. Several weeks later he was sent back to Canada for the rest of his rehabilitation. Sims was able to return to our unit three months later, just before our mission to Mexico City.

Caloway and myself, caught up with Johns back at the Mogadishu airport where all of us caught a flight back to Germany. We traded a few stories about the mission, ate, drank and fell asleep and didn't wake up until the Load Master kicked me in Germany. We then parted ways with our comrades for this mission.

After the success of our mission NATO, (North Atlantic Treaty Organization) and the UN (United Nations) decided to create a rapid response task force that could be inserted into any location on the planet within twenty four hours to perform special operations (Spec Ops). Special operations could be hostage retrieval,

assassinations, really any job that could need special

attention. Many countries had organizations such as the American SEALs and the British SAS; however, there were none that fell under NATO or UN Command. The world was becoming more and more a destabilized place and missions like this one were only going to grow in their complexity over larger geographic areas.

Two months after our return to Germany we were reunited with our comrades from this mission to begin forming the WWRRF (World Wide Rapid Response Force). The twenty of us from the Somalia mission all volunteered to become the first members. We were tested and retested by some of the most elite trainers in the world. We helped develop the curriculum for the program and set the standards that recruit members would have to adhere to. Because this force was to be worldwide, the training was very elaborate. Members became highly trained specialists in desert, mountain, jungle and urban warfare and were trained to be inserted from the air, sea, and land. In time I would become the Task Force Commander, but not until I had completed many, many missions, some successful, some not.

Part 2

In the Beginning

I turn to see my wife fully asleep. I turn over and look at my alarm clock, it's 0612, that is two hours later than I usually sleep. Lying on my side I look out the patio door and up the hill to see the cows grazing. The summer flowers are in full bloom now and the smell is wonderful. A gentle breeze blows the curtains. The summer sun is high in the sky already and I can see the light dance off the pool and reflect on the bedroom ceiling. I think about the water, is it cold or warm? I take a deep breath and sigh. It is great to be in my own bed, I had forgotten how wonderful it is just to be home.

My wife stirs beside me. I don't want to wake her; she never gets to sleep in. I don't hear any kids yet. They will be up two seconds after they hear me. I don't move a muscle. I look back out the patio door. It is open halfway and the screen makes a whistling sound as the wind passes by. Sweet air fills the room. I drift back to sleep.

An hour and a half has past. My eyes open slowly. I look at my clock again it's 0745, still no kids. Maybe they don't know I'm home. I see a bee fly past the door as it makes its summer rounds. I see the reflection of the pool water on the ceiling again. I think to myself, "Just jump in the pool." I have been wanting to ever since I got back to Canada. I spring out of bed, go over to the door fling it open and close it quickly behind me; two steps and I am in the pool. Splash. Now the whole house is awake.

"Dad's home, dad's home," they yell and come running out to the pool. "Get in," I urge. I only have to say it once and all three of them jump in and swim over to me. They all hug me in the water and I get many kisses from each of them. "What did you bring us?" the oldest one Seth asks. "I wasn't out shopping," I explained. "I know what I can give you, how about a big hug and a kiss?." They all maul me at once and I love it. If there is one thing I am sure of it is that absence makes the heart grow fonder. Whenever I'm on a mission I try to not think about them because I miss them all too much.

"Come on, let's have a splash battle," says our three year old daughter Nexas. The kid swims like she was born in water. They all swim better than me. I never got a chance to swim growing up in the city. There was a pool near where we lived, but my mother and father put more influence on studying than any physical pursuits. We spent more time with computers and android tutors than our parents. Some days we would go outside and hide just to get out for a couple of hours. I swore to myself that my children were never going to have the life I had. My kids were going to go outside and play and have the type of childhood I dreamed of.

We splash away in the pool for over an hour, half clothed, half naked. My wife comes to the door a couple of times just to look at us. I smile at her. Kim is not just my wife she is my best friend. The one person that understands who I am, why I do the things I do. I love her more every day, and I can't imagine my life without my rock.

After playing very hard and getting more than a little tired I smell bacon. Not the vegetable modified strips of artificial bacon, but real bacon. There must be eggs and toast too. "Hey guys I smell food," I say in a hurry to get out of the pool. "Me too," says our seven year old Broan. This kid is always hungry like me. Just as he says that

Kim calls us for breakfast. We jump out of the pool and dry off. I send the kids off to get dressed.

We all meet back in the kitchen. The smell is wonderful. Living in the country really has it perks. We have a huge garden in the back where I grow all of our vegetables and apples and pears. We have many local farmers that sell us beef and chicken and pork. We don't have to eat the packaged crap the rest of the 9 billion people in the world have to eat. We get first pick of all the best foods and we are grateful for what we have.

Kim has made fried potatoes and bacon and sausage. There is a bowl of fresh fruit from the garden with grapes and watermelon and lots of pears and strawberries. The toast is covered with butter and there is orange or cranberry juice to drink. I look at the food with wonderment. I sit down and help Nexas fill her plate. The two boys are already eating. They all smile not because of the food but because we are all home together. No one says a word, we just eat together for the first time in weeks. This is what I miss when I am away. My family means more to me than anything in this world.

Although I miss them while I am away I know that what I do keeps the United North America safe and in turn keeps my family safe. My kids don't know what I do and I don't want them to know. They know their father is in the military, and that is all they need to know. My wife knows better than to ask me about where I go or what I do. She knows it's dangerous; she also knows I am one of the best in the world at what I do. I think that gives her some confidence when I am away.

I help clean up the kitchen and the kids head outside. Kim and I are alone for the first time in weeks. "So how did you make out?" she asks me. "I'm OK, but Sims got hurt bad," I say with some remorse. I turn away as a great sadness fills me up. "Oh no, will he be alright?" she asks. "He will be, but he was hit twice, it will take him a long time to get back." I try to choke back the tears. Kim comes over and hugs me. I hug her back. I think about Sims and his family. I know I have to call his wife and parents. I have to get up the courage and I have to do it soon. "I have to go and call his wife and parents, I'll go downstairs to do it, I'll be right back up," I tell Kim. She hugs me tighter and I head downstairs.

I turn on my computer for the first time in weeks. It greets me and I ask it to turn on Skype and call Molly Sims, Terry Sims wife. Molly Sims' number rings and rings and no one answers. I ask the computer to call Greg Sims, Terry's father. It rings and he picks up right away. The video starts up quickly, but before it opens I answer, "Hi Greg," I await his reply. "Hi Zeke how are you?" he asks. "I'm fine I am calling about Terry," I reply. "He's still in Germany, I talked to him yesterday he says you saved his life, Hi Zeke it's Molly," she interrupts. "Hi Molly I just called your house, how you holding up?" I ask. She smiles at me, "Thanks for what you did, Terry says you're his hero," she says thanking me. "I'm no hero," I state. "Well Terry says you are," says Greg.

I don't feel like much of a hero. One of my best friends got shot twice because of a decision I made. I feel like shit not a hero. These people think I'm a fuckin' war hero and all I do is feel like crying. Some fuckin' hero!

"Did you talk to him today?" I ask. "No it was yesterday, he had another surgery on his leg today. He should be back in Canada on Monday he thinks," Molly states. "Hi

Rod Bergeron

Zeke how are you holding up?" Sims mother asks. "Oh, I'm ok how about you?" I ask. "Oh don't worry about us, you go and spend some time with your family. We'll call you when we hear from him, or you call us if you hear from him, OK?" she asks. "OK. Well I'll let you go, you call me if you hear anything, please," I beg. "We will, take care," Molly closes. I turn Skype off.

I sit for a second and think about Sims. He is probably causing havoc at the hospital; he always was a shit disturber. I take comfort in the fact that his family doesn't blame me, even though I blame myself. It's not a good feeling. I know I will be there for him and his family when he gets back.

I have to think about my family right now and that they need me. I stand and turn to walk up the stairs. I get to the top stair and hear the kids outside playing. I go over to the door and look out at my kids playing in the backyard. The laughter, the fun, the freedom of childhood, it's almost too much to take.

I go to my bedroom and get dressed go back down the hall

and look for my shoes. They are not there. I go back to my bedroom and look under the bed. They are there and I pull them out. I stick my foot in and feel something inside. I take the shoe off and feel inside. There is a candy with a little note on it that says "Daddy". I sit and cry. I don't know why, but I just sit and cry. I guess they miss me when I'm gone. I thought they didn't. I mean I hoped they didn't. I pull myself back together again and head outside to play in the warm sun with the kids.

We play and I forget about Sims and the other guys and Somalia even if it's only just for a while. We go in for lunch and then head back out to the pool. My parents come over to see me and the kids and Kim's mother comes over as well. We sit around the pool and have a nice time and enjoy a nice bottle of wine my mother has brought. I am somewhat distant. Distracted but trying to stay in the moment. I know it's the last mission that is bothering me but I have to move past it.

I start the barbeque and warm it up. We have some huge sirloin steaks and some burgers for the kids. I take the steaks off the plate and put them on the barbeque and they immediately sizzle; a wonderful smell rises up and fills the entire pool area. I turn to take the plate in and see a small pool of blood on the plate and I freeze. My mind goes immediately to Sims. I can't get the sight of his blood out of my mind. The people we killed don't bother me nor their blood but Sims blood, that bothers me. I snap back and smile and hand the plate to Kim on her way in. The rest of that day I feel distant, not connected somehow. After dinner we all watch a movie and then get the kids in bed. Kim and I go to bed and hug and cuddle and do what adults do. I wake in the morning and feel completely anew. "It's a new day," I think to myself. I look outside to see another beautiful day greet me. I stand in the patio doorway and let the warm sun heat up my face and chest and abdomen. I close my eyes and just let the sun bathe my body. The phone rings and I'm jerked back to reality. "Oh who the fuck can this be so early in the morning?" I say to know one. I pick up the phone.

I look at the call display, an overseas call from Morton. I immediately think Colonel Morton, the Brit. "No it can't be," I think to myself. "Hello," I say. "Hello and good morning, could I speak with Lieutenant Heron?" he asks with a pleasing British accent. "Good morning Colonel Morton, how are you on this very fine day?" I ask politely. "I am quite well indeed, do you have a few moments for the phone?" he inquires. "Yes of course," I state. "I am going to switch us over to secure channel, just a moment please." He wants to secure our communications so that no one else can hear what we are talking about. I think right away that there is trouble somewhere, maybe back in Somalia. I think maybe he is calling me for a mission somewhere. I take a deep breathe.

"There we go, alright then. It seems we have impressed some people with the last mission we completed," he offers. "I think we impressed ourselves to some degree. We were quick and efficient and were able to take on a second tasking with no prep and down more than twenty five percent of our personnel," I state. "Yes it is pretty impressive when you say it like that isn't it?" he adds. With the exception of our two wounded we did a lot of work in a very short period of time not to mention we saved a whole squad of guys from a helicopter.

"Yes well some of the higher ups have recognized the

speed and accuracy of that mission and would like us to try to work together on a more permanent basis," he states quickly. "They seem to think that the Americans, Canadians and we Brits should put together a task force for future operations. They are looking for volunteers and asked me if I would enquire with you and your team," he says. "Under who would this taskforce be commanded, who would we report to and receive orders from?" I ask curiously.

"Well Lieutenant Heron, all of the details have not been worked out yet," Colonel Morton said cautiously. "And we have not yet figured out who the team might consist of or where any actual training may take place; however, the Americans have offered us a training area in Texas. Of course all the details are still to be worked out. Right now I am just trying to see who may be interested. So you take some time and give it some consideration," he suggested.

I thought for a second, "Yes I think I would like some time to think this over, could I get back to you in a couple of days." "Certainly, I will give you a call in a couple of days, meanwhile I will send you some of the preliminary material that I have received for you to review, it just outlines the types of missions and assets that would be at our disposal," he states. "Oh, that would be great, who is this from?" I ask. "This is a NATO document and it is marked secret so I will send it to you securely." he replies. "Certainly, I understand, I look forward to talking to you in a few days," I suggest. "Alright then have a great day," the Colonel closes. "You have a great day too Colonel," I close off.

I sit in my hard chair thinking about what just happened. Is this an opportunity that I want to pursue or is it going to be a huge commitment that will take me away from my family for long periods of time? Texas is only four and a half hours away by military aircraft and certainly a couple of hours closer than Germany. Most of the missions I have done in the last couple of years have all originated from Germany, it's where the largest NATO base in Europe is. If I took this job I could fly out of Trenton Air Base which is only twenty five minutes from home.

My ass is starting to hurt in this chair and it is a beautiful summer day, I need to get out and do something. I stand and stretch and look towards the ceiling. My back cracks as I stretch and every little pain and ache becomes even more apparent. Am I too old for this?

I think for a second before I head upstairs. How am I going to explain this to Kim? Do I even want to do it? I like the people I work with now. I like my colonel, Colonel Rodd. I get along really well with everyone and I am basically allowed to do anything I want. I know all the bases I work out of like the back of my hand and I really like being able to make up my own schedule. But a change might be good. Some new training with some really elite guys might make me and my team better. I am going to go and enjoy this day and I'll talk to Kim about it later.

We spend the day with the kids and have fun in the pool and just hanging around the house. Later in the evening we get the kids to bed and I finally get a minute to talk to Kim. "You know that call I took this morning," I ask. "Yeah, I heard you talking to someone. I thought maybe it was something about Terry," she states. "Oh no it was nothing about Terry it was this British Colonel I worked with," I state. "Was he calling about another mission so soon?" she asks. "Oh nothing about a mission, I still have three weeks off. He was enquiring with me about a new team", I state enthusiastically. She comes over to me and looks me right in the face. "Someone is always wanting you for some team that ends up taking you away from us," she states passionately. I turn to her and put both of my hands on her waist and look her in the eye. "The work I do is very important and I would not be asked to do it if it wasn't absolutely necessary," I state directly. "I don't know anything about it right now other than my team and I have been asked to join or at least consider joining," I put to her.

"I think this may be an opportunity for me to stay in North America on a more permanent basis. The training area would be in Texas, and that is all I know right now," I say encouragingly. "Why does it always have to be you, is there really no one else?" Kim pleads. "You know what we do is difficult and the training is highly specialized. There are very few people that can do what I do, what any of us do," I hold her tighter. "Let's not worry about it until I see what it is all about OK?" I ask. "OK let's wait and see," Kim agrees.

For the remainder of that day I tried to stay focused on the kids and Kim and not let any of what was going on take me away from them. I had missed them and they had missed me; it was not fair of me to mentally be away while I was physically here. We had a great day out by the pool and looking for butterflies in the fields. That night we had a campfire in the backyard and all in all had a great day.

I woke up early and crept down to my computer before anyone else was awake. I told my computer to turn on and check for new messages. The first message was from Colonel Morton. I was excited and afraid all at the same time. The computer warned me that the message was marked Top Secret and was marked Your Eyes Only, which simply means keep this to yourself and it will automatically be removed from your computer once you have had some time to review it. Usually that meant you may have several hours or days depending upon the size of the file, this was only three pages.

It began with all of the niceties like date and time of creation and that it was from the Joint Task Force, United Nations and NATO. It described the need for a rapid deployment Task Force that could be deployed anywhere in the world within minutes of a situation requiring an immediate response. What these situations would be was not disclosed; however, I had a feeling it was situations like Somalia. The training was described as broad and deep with all current training methods being used. The equipment was described as innovative and experimental in nature. For me that meant that we were going to have access to all of the best stuff to blow shit up; for an infantry guy that is like Christmas and your birthday all wrapped up together. The best physical and psychological trainers were already employed to begin with selection and recruitment.

We were being asked to assist with developing training protocols and setting standards for selection and recruitment. We would also be involved with taking new recruits out to field test them in real life situations and develop their skills further. The assignment was to take the current group of five teams of four to twenty teams of four within two years. For me this is the shit I live for, I was born to do this type of work. I love teaching and I love fighting and this is a job that would allow me to do both. To me the only stumbling block is that it is in Texas, fuckin' Texas. How do I swing doing this and being with my family?

I delete the message and sit and think. I wonder if there is any way I can wrangle my own schedule. I will have to talk to Colonel Morton. Maybe I should just email him at least that way I get it in writing. Yeah, that is what I will do, just email him and ask the questions. I sit at the computer and dictate my message.

Marked Confidential and Classified Secret
Hello Colonel Morton
Thank you for sending me the message yesterday. I have reviewed it and I have but one question. I fully understand that the particulars of this team are not fully set yet.

Is it possible that my current team is allowed to stay with me? I have trained and fought with these men for several years now and we have become a very close knit team. I would like to continue working with them.

Please feel free to contact me about any of these matters at your leisure.

Thanking you in advance.

Lt. Heron

I read the message twice and sent it off. I wondered if I asked for what I wanted. Do I really want to be a part of this team? I continue to question myself. I think this will be a great step up for both me and my team. Will the others want to do this? I stand to walk away and my computer tells me I have an incoming message from Colonel Morton. I tell the computer to display the message and I sit up straight in my chair to read it.

Marked Confidential and Classified Secret
Good Morning Lt. Heron

I believe you have raised some points that have already been brought up by my very own men. You must understand that I am not going to be in command of this taskforce. As of now I am only in a position to ask for volunteers.

As for teams, of course you would stay with your current team members for any training and missions. I don't believe anyone would want to mess with a team of your calibre.

If these answers are sufficient for you I would encourage you to contact your team members to ask about their interest in the Task Force. We would like to begin testing and training in two weeks. The initial testing will require four days.

If you have any further question please feel free to contact me.

Colonel Morton

I think about this message for a moment. I feel satisfied that I will be able to satisfy the needs of my family and my team. If I can't, then I will just return my team back to our original postings. I still have not talked to anyone on my team. If they are not willing to go, then I won't want to take part either.

As soon as I start to think about my team I think about

Sims. "T" as we call him which is short for Terry. I don't think most people even know his name. I wonder how he is. I tell my computer to call Terry's wife and there is no answer. Then I tell the computer to call Terry's parents and the line is busy. I wait again and it rings and Terry's mother quickly answers. "Hi there Zeke is that you?" she asks before the video even starts up. "Hi Cindy, oh I can see you now," I say. "How are you today?" I ask. "Oh we are great. We just heard from Terry, he is fine and is going to Peterborough General Hospital today," she says cheerfully. "Oh that is great, he'll be close then," I state. "Can I still call him now or is he already gone," I ask. "He said he was leaving shortly, so I don't know. Do you want to come with us to see him tomorrow?" Cindy asks. "Oh no, you spend some time with him tomorrow and I'll go up the next day, I'm sure Molly wants to have some time with him," I state. "Are you sure? You know you are welcome to come with us," Cindy says. "Yes I'm sure, I'll go up on Tuesday, I'll send him a message right now," I say. "OK Zeke, we'll tell him you'll see him soon," Cindy says. "OK you have a good day now," I close. "Bye Zeke see you soon," Cindy closes.

Rod Bergeron

I think to myself that I had better wait to ask Sims if he wants to join the taskforce. I am almost sure he would be the first to go; but, for his sake I had better wait until he has had a chance to recover. I figure it will be months before he can even train again, if ever. I think it is better to go and ask Kim what she thinks before I move ahead at all. If she thinks we can do it as a family then I will start to ask the others. I cannot move ahead without her blessing, it just would not be right.

I get out of my chair and head upstairs wondering if anyone is awake yet. Kim is just coming down the hall. "Hi Hun," she says as she gives me a kiss. "I heard you down there talking, was it Terry?" she asks. "No, it was his mother; they are moving him to Peterborough today, I said I would go up and see him in a couple of days," I say. "Oh that's nice. Any word from the Colonel?" she asks. "Yeah he sent me a message," I reply. I wait to formulate my answer. "Well was it what you wanted?" she asks. "Actually it was," I give a little smile. "Well, are you keeping it a secret or are you going to tell?" she asks. "Yeah well basically he said all of his guys asked the same questions. He said he is not in charge of the unit but that time off is definitely going to be a major consideration," I state flatly. "Well do you think you want to go?" she asks. "I'm not going unless the rest of the guys want to do it too; I'm going to call all of them today and see what they think of the idea," I state flatly again. "So when would you start then?" is her reply. "They want to start testing and training in two weeks, but there was no exact date," I say. "Will Terry be ready by then?" she asks. "No, he will have to start later," I say. "Well as long as you still have two weeks off, let's have some fun," she says cheerfully.

Later that day I got ahold of Gord Johns and Chris Caloway and gave them the information I had received from Colonel Morton. They were more than enthusiastic about the prospect of joining the taskforce. I went to the Peterborough hospital the next day to see Terry only to discover that Caloway had already told him of the taskforce. I guess I didn't tell him not to tell Terry. Terry was also very much interested and said as soon as he was feeling up to it he would join us in Texas. Three weeks later he joined us fully recovered and still very fit.

In the middle of August my orders finally came through. I was to report to Trenton with my team, with the exception of Sims, "T", and command of our unit was to be turned over to WWRRF (World Wide Rapid Response Force). I met my guys in the terminal at Trenton Air Base. Everyone looked very much rested and a little jittery like a bunch of kids on the first day of school. We boarded our flight and five hours later we arrived in Texas.

Part 3

A Whole New World

We landed on a small air strip in the middle of no where. There were two hangers and two small, one story buildings, a lot of rock and sand with some forested areas off in the distance. The sun burned brightly and there was not a cloud in the sky. Our plane set down and we could see a bunch of people standing in the one hanger door. We taxied around and stopped just in front of the hanger. The plane door opened and we jumped out and grabbed our equipment from the belly of the plane. We walked over to where the others were standing and saw our colleagues from Somalia.

"Holy fuck look what the cat dragged in!" exclaims one of the Americans. "How and the fuck are you bunch of assholes?" I say. Then we are greeted with handshakes and more foul language. Colonel Morton greets me. "Lieutenant Heron bring your men and equipment, I'll show you to your quarters," he says. We follow him into the closest building and to the rear where there is an elevator. I think to myself, "Where are we going? This place is all underground." We get into the elevator, which is huge, and start down. There are twenty two floors, all underground. When the doors open we are in a very well lit, huge, dorm like room. There are bunks, chairs, tables, desk, televisions and lots of open area.

"Your team is down there," the Colonel points down the row of bunks. I nod to him in agreement. "There are orders there for you, read them and get ready. You have thirty minutes," he says. I drop my equipment and pick up a letter with my name on the front. I open mine and the other two open theirs. I start to read it and Caloway pipes in. "Oh, it's a welcome letter how nice," he says. I ignore him and read my letter.

Hello Lt. Heron

Welcome to the WWRRF (World Wide Rapid Response Force) testing and training centre. Your acceptance to this program is conditional upon completion of the testing phase.

The testing phase will take place over the next four days and it is mandatory that all phases be completed and passed in order to be selected for the WWRRF. If any one area is failed, only one retest will be allowed. If that retest is unsuccessful, you will be asked to leave the facility immediately.

Please dress for a ruck march and report immediately to the upper level. Weapons and other equipment will be distributed before the march begins.

Best of Luck
General Fitch

I wonder who General Fitch is. "Is this going to be like basic all over again?" Johns asks. "I have no idea, let's just go with it and see what happens," I state. "What are you taking Lt?" Caloway asks. "I'm going to change my socks, underwear and T-shirt," I say. "Yeah I'm going to do the same," says Johns. We all change and grab a quick drink and get into the elevator and go back up. Everyone is quiet. I'm not too sure what to expect. As the elevator door opens we are immediately hit by the heat. It is a very dry desert heat.

We walk towards the hanger and see everyone still hanging around. We walk in and are immediately called over to a seating area. Colonel Morton gets our attention. A man I do not know steps to the front. "I am General Fitch, formally of the second Mountain Division Army Rangers. I will be the commander of WWRRF. I was chosen by NATO and the UN. I am not your usual General. I don't sit on my ass and let others do my work for me. I get dirty just like all of you. I consider myself to be in the company of some of the most elite soldiers on the planet and I look forward to learning from each of you," Fitch introduces himself.

"Over the next couple of days you will be tested to your limits. These tests are not only to test your skills but to help us determine the skills that will be required by future WWRRF recruits. You men get to help set the standards. Listen closely to the directions given. You are being assessed here as individuals, there are no points for helping one another. If someone is in trouble one of our staff will assist them it is not your responsibility," he states. Off to his right there is a group of twelve people. He introduces them as the training staff. Some of them are doctors and other medical staff, some are weapons technicians and others are martial arts trainers and physical training staff.

"Behind you is the equipment you will require for the beginning of these tests. Each group of equipment is exactly the same. Choose your equipment and I will now turn you over to Captain Fields. Best of luck to all of you," he concludes.

"I am Captain Fields I will be in charge of physical standards. Today we are going to be testing speed and agility on a long rough course. I will not be divulging the length of the course only to say it is long. You will find many stations along the way and you will be subjected to several physical exams by the medical staff along the route. Please gather your equipment and we will have a mass start in five minutes," Fields says.

I choose a pile of equipment: a rucksack, which is army for backpack and a CQ4 rifle, one of my favourites. I don't bother to look in the pack. I don't really care what is in it. I take to heart what Captain Fields just said about this being a long march over rough terrain with little or no breaks. I've done this many times before and I am more than fit enough to do this. I just hope that my guys got enough rest before they came here. I know Johns hates this shit. I look at him and he rolls his eyes. I know he can do this, I just wonder if he knows it. "Stick together," I say to Johns and Caloway. They both nod. The Americans also hear me and look to their leaders and they also nod.

"Two minutes," Captain Fields says. "Remember you are all being marked as individuals, there are no points for helping each other," he says. I think to myself, "You are talking to a group of guys who work together all the time; telling them to not help each other out just won't work." I grab a bottle of water from a nearby case and stick it into my cargo pocket on my pants. I grab a second bottle and drink half of it and take off my wide brimmed hat. I pour the other half of the bottle into my hat and swirl it around as I watch it soak into the material. I grab two energy bars from a box and stick them into my shirt pocket. "One minute," Captain Fields says. We all line up outside the hanger. "Follow the marked path the entire way. Begin," he says. We are off with a fast walk and we are all together. No one says a word until we are out of sight.

In the first couple of steps Colonel Morton catches up to me. We look at each other and smile. We are near the front of the group with only three Americans in front of us. We follow a row of tall trees that have red plastic tape tied around them as the markers. We walk as an undisciplined group for about ten steps and then our training kicks in and we are all walking single file with about five metres between each of us, just as we have always been taught.

After walking about two kilometres Colonel Morton calls us all to a halt. He gathers us all around. "OK guys, I don't know about the rest of you but I know we are stronger as a group than we are as individual units," he suggest. "I don't think they really believe that we are going to work as separate teams. Who knows what they have planned. Let's keep our eyes and ears open and see what they throw at us. Alright?" he asks. We all agree. "We have no ammo right?" one of the Americans asks. Everyone shakes their heads, no. "So why the weapons?" I ask. "Who the fuck knows," says a voice in the crowd. "Let's move, keep your eyes and ears open," Colonel Morton suggest.

One of the Americans takes the lead. My team and I are at the rear. We all keep our five metre spacing and move steadily and quietly. The hot midday sun beats down hard on us. My clothes are soaked with sweat and I can feel my once wet hat dry onto my head. The path we are on is rough stone and there are a few blades of tough grass between the rocks. I look at my boots and see they are covered with the sand we march on. We march on this rough path for over an hour before the lead man holds his fist high for all to see, bringing us to a quick halt. Everyone kneels down. We all check the sides around us just as we have all been taught to do so many times.

I crouch down and move up to the front to see what is there. We look down into a small valley near a trickling stream. There are four men milling around a couple of tables with what looks like weapons on them. I have no binoculars to get a closer look. They do not seem to have been alerted to our presence or maybe they don't care. I go back and tell the other leaders what is ahead and we collectively decide to just walk in. We stay in line and walk into the valley down a steep path to the bottom. We follow the path over to the men and they tell us to stop.

A man with a very fit and muscled face comes up to us. "Drop your shit, you are going to do a pistol range exercise," he commands. No one has any rank on so we don't really know what to call them. In the military if someone does not have rank on to distinguish themselves you automatically assume they are an officer. Luckily they don't really seem to care what rank we are either. "Three at a time go up to the range and fire ten shots at a stationary target ten metres to your front. Move quickly," he orders. In quick succession we all load a pistol, hit the targets and get our equipment back on. We all pass and are told to continue on the marked path.

About three kilometres from the pistol range there are two people ahead standing on a ridge. I am near the front and I get signalled from the lead man to stop. I go up to him and he is pointing at people standing around. I go back and call the leaders up once again and we decide to move up. As we approach the two men, they begin to yell and scream at us as we pass. "You were told to act alone," one says. "Get fucking moving, you should have been done already!" screams the other. "Maybe we got sent the wrong people, you assholes are slow as fuck," the first one says. I smile and look them right in the face. So does

Rod Bergeron

everyone else. "What the fuck you looking at asshole?" the second man says. We just keep on walking. I think to myself, "Fuck are we back in basic training?" These dicks wouldn't scare one of my kids.

For the first time I pull out my bottle of water and take a small drink. I see others have already finished their water. The sun is beginning to set. I call the group to a halt and we all gather. I take my rucksack off and sit on it. "Break time?" someone asks. "You got it," someone responds. We are along a riverbed with a small river beside us. The area we are sitting on is flat and sandy. The sun is low in the sky and we have about one hour of day light left.

"Hey look at this," I hear someone say. I look over to see someone going through their rucksack and pulling stuff out. I look at Frank one of the Americans. "Anyone ever look in their ruck?" he asks. I shake my head no. We all open our rucksacks and are surprised. They all have socks, a rain coat that could be used as a shelter, rope, two bottles of water, water purification tablets and three energy bars. Colonel Morton comes over to us. "Want to camp here or keep going tonight?" he asks. Frank asks, "We don't have any night vision gear do we?" "I don't," I say. "Fuck it then let's just camp, set up some houches and get some sleep," says Frank. "Let's do it. We have been on the move for twelve hours now. My team and I started this day two days ago," says Colonel Morton. "Listen up," he calls to everyone, "We are going to stay here tonight". "Set up some shelters and get some sleep. Set up some patrols and a couple of listening posts. You know what to do," he finishes.

The men quickly talk things over and decide who will do what. They make up teams of people to do the listening posts and the patrols and decide who will switch and at what time. Half of the teams will sleep while the other half does the patrols and listening posts. With most military operations it is standard procedure to have someone far from the camp listening for intruders and groups patrolling while the remaining members of the group get some rest. I say, "get some rest", because seldom do I ever actually fall asleep. Sometimes I fall over from exhaustion; but, seldom do I sleep while on any type of operation.

I go over to a sandy patch of land under one of the only trees. I get out my rope and my shelter and set my houch. I always make mine very low to ground and this time is no different. The air is beginning to cool and there are dark clouds on the horizon. I think we are in for some rain tonight. We are all set up against the dry, sandy shore of the river under the only trees around. Some logs are brought over to sit on and we all start to eat and drink. After some food and water I am ready for bed. The guys have already decided who was going to take what shifts and I was not on the list. Thank Christ.

I head off to bed, which is a few straight dry logs set side-by-side under my shelter. I take off my boots and pull my rucksack under my head. The logs are hard under me but I'm so tired I won't mind. I take my shirt off and lay it over my body as my only blanket. I close my eyes but sleep does not come easily. There are still a couple of voices around and someone yells to them to shut up. I agree, if only in my mind. My thoughts drift to home and I think of my wife and kids. I miss them. I am lying on a couple of hard logs rather than my soft bed. What is wrong with me? Why do I do this? Sleep never comes.

When the first light is seen in the sky I hear someone digging through their rucksack. I stretch while I am still lying down. I stick my head out to see guys eating and drinking and just sitting around shooting the shit. It's more like a Boy Scout camp than a military exercise. I put on a fresh pair of socks and put my boots back on. I always tie my boots the same way, like they may not be off for a long time. I crawl out and take down my shelter. I grab an energy bar and eat it with some water. I fill my bottle with stream water and put one of my water purification tablets in and shake it up. I scoop up a couple of handfuls of water and wash my face and hands. I dip my hat into the water then ring it out and place it back onto my head. I wipe my hands on my pants to dry them.

The sun is barely up in the sky but it is already getting warm out.

A couple of kilometres down the trail we run into another station. This time it is a first aid test. "You fuckin' assholes had might as well pack your shit and go home. You were suppose to be here yesterday," says one of the testers. I smile and so does everyone else. They do not look happy. Too fucking bad. We are given a scenario and asked to do first aid on a couple of dummies. We complete the task in just a couple of minutes, allowing our medical persons to take the lead and the rest of us provided a perimeter and assisted with the stretchers. We are subjected to a urine and blood test and we were soon off again.

We follow the marked trail down a narrow valley. Around a bend in the trail we come across several houses, a small barn and a couple of other buildings. It looks like a raggedy ass little village. There are several staff members there that we now recognize and we walk over to meet them. We are told that this is a hostage recovery drill. There are civilians, the hostage, as well as hostage takers. All of the hostage takers are dummies and should be eliminated. There are to be no civilian casualties. Any civilian casualty will be considered a failure. The civilians are also dummies. We were going to be monitored by closed circuit television. We are given five minutes to plan and are told we have three minutes to rescue the hostage.

The other leaders and I gather and start to draw our plans up in the dirt with a stick. We decide to stay in our five groups. The one British team has the most training and experience in hostage retrieval so they will take the job of finding and retrieving the hostage. One American team will circle to the right, clearing the buildings as they come to them, and the other American team will circle to the left. Our team and the other British team are going into the centre to take the one large barn and act as backup in case something goes horribly wrong.

We are given live ammunition and communications gear as well as body armour. We gear up and are brought to a starting line. Once again we are warned that we are the only living people in these buildings. There is medical staff on site. We all test our communications gear and it works properly.

To make this as difficult as possible, it is only two thirty in the afternoon, so we don't have the cover of darkness or the element of surprise. We are lucky that there are no live people in these buildings or it would be much more difficult. We move into position to begin and are given the word to start.

The American teams move out first, making a far sweeping arch off to each side. They move at a full sprint. I am impressed. Sprinting after being out here this long with little food or water is impressive. The main hostage retrieval team moves up the road directly into the village using old cars and trucks as cover. Our team and the other British team move right behind them. The American teams radio that they are moving in from the right and the left towards their first building. The main British team has reached the first building to their front and have cleared the building and there is no hostage, they move on. One minute has passed. My team and the second British team get to the barn. My team goes to the right and the British guys go left. We all go in at the same time. Nothing. I run up the ladder into the hay loft and again nothing. We radio the others that the barn is clear. Both American teams radio that their buildings are clear and then move on. We hold our position and create a defensive perimeter. Two minutes have passed. Within a couple of seconds the Brits radio that the hostage is safe and the targets are down. The Brits rush past us with the hostage in tow and it is over, just like that.

We all take off our body armour and throw it into a pile. I take a big drink and put my gear back on. We all smile at each other. Someone in the group says to the training staff, "Let me know when this is going to start getting difficult will ya." A bit of a smart ass comment, but true none the less.

Another couple of kilometres go by and we are stopped for blood and urine samples again. We are given some water and energy bars and we are soon off again. If I eat any more energy bars I am going to puke. They give you lots of energy but are hard to live on for a couple of days. I guess that is all part of the test. A few more kilometres down the trail and we come upon a rifle range. The day goes on like this through the hot sun until at about 5:00 pm we are back at the base. We have more blood and urine tests as soon as we are back. A group of medical persons check our hearts and respiration. We all go to the mess and eat everything we can and then head for the showers. I let the warm water run over me and I almost fall asleep. I head back to my dorm and fall exhausted into my bunk.

The next morning we are all summoned to a meeting in our dorm. The staff is all assembled and General Fitch comes to the front. "Good morning, I take it you all had a reasonable amount of rest. I am most pleased with the outcome of the past couple of days. You acted as I had hoped, one cohesive unit. You resisted acting as individuals and completed all of the tasks above our expectations. You truly are a fit bunch. We are going to spend today familiarizing you with some of the equipment we have here, as well as, look at some of the weapons we are privileged to have. If there are no questions I will have you divide into your own sections and go with one of the four trainers." We all look at each other and no one has any questions. "Alright then, away you go," he adds.

I catch up with Johns and Caloway and we introduce ourselves to our trainer. His name is Brook Timins. Brook takes us to the elevator and we go down two levels to the weapons section. He swipes his ID at the door and a buzzer goes off and the door opens. We go through a second locked door and we are in. The room is long and wide. There is a weapons lockup on one side and six long firing ranges. There is a large open area in the middle set up like a classroom with a whiteboard and chairs. Brook takes us over to the weapons lockup and swipes his card again and the gate opens.

There are a lot of weapons, more than lots of weapons. Some are very familiar and some I have never seen before.

We systematically go through all of the most common weapons from all over the globe. We look at weapons from China, Russia, Great Britain and North America. All of which we are very familiar with. We look at handguns, as well as, rifles, machine guns and grenade launchers. Brook asks each of us questions to assure that we are familiar with each weapon. We are asked to fire five rounds of various weapons in order for him to gauge our level of understanding and skill. Once he was assured of our knowledge we move on to some weapons that we had never seen or heard of.

"What we have here is an energy weapon," he pulls a short rifle off the shelf. The rifle has a normal size stock, but everything else is different. There is no opening for a barrel and where the barrel opening should be there is a triangular black box about twenty centimetres long. There are two small cables that run from the triangular box to the stock on both sides. "This is a fifth generation energy weapon. It has been in development for over ten years. This task force will be the first NATO group to have access to this weapon, the CEWG5 (Concentrated Energy Weapon Generation 5). The premise is quite simple. The weapon fires a pulse of energy that, depending upon how it is configured, will either kill or incapacitate an enemy. The weapon has a wide range of energy projectiles, from a wide burst to a very fine single pinpoint," Brook explains. We look at him and this weapon with amazement. "So it's like a laser," Johns asks. "No, not really, a laser uses concentrated light and this weapon fires an invisible energy. Not only does it not fire a projectile, but there are no rounds to carry, no muzzle flash to give you away, all you carry are back up batteries. Two of these batteries will fire over two thousand times," he continues.

"Holy fuck," Caloway says. Caloway reaches for the weapon and Brook hands it to him. He hefts it in his hands and nods. "Light as fuck," he says. We are all a little stunned. "What else do you got?" Johns asks. Brook turns to the drawers and pulls out a handgun that looks exactly the same. There is a small triangular box where the muzzle should be and the rest of it looks like a handgun. Brook hands it to Johns. "Fuck me," he looks at it like a kid that just got his first pellet gun. "Let's go over to the range," he says. We follow him over.

Brook takes two batteries and plugs them into the rear of
the stock. A green light comes on at the top of the stock.
He points the weapon downrange at the targets. "The main
problem with this weapon is there is no noise, no
kickback, the only way you know it was fired is that the
person you fired it at is dead," he says. "Look at the
target," he raises the weapon to his shoulder, points it
downrange and fires. A small hole appears in the middle
of the target. He then aims at the left of the target fires and
moves the weapon to the right and the target falls to the
ground, cut in half. "Holy Fuck," Calloway says. "Let me
try this," Johns pushes past me to get at the weapon.
Brook hands it to him. "I had a feeling you might like it,"
Brook says. Johns puts the weapon up to his shoulder and
Brook shows him the two stage safety. He fires and he
smiles ear to ear.

Johns fires at the target to the right and slices it right in
half. Next he fires a couple of burst at the target and puts a
happy face on it. He smiles again ear to ear. Brook takes
the weapon and makes a couple of changes to the two
small knobs by the trigger. Johns shoulders the weapon
again and fires and the target has hundreds of small holes
like a shotgun would make. "Holy shit, what a piece of

equipment. Can I get one of those?" he asks. "Once you have been fully trained you can have one," Brook says. "I'll show you some of its features and limitations. First it will go through paper targets easily, it will also go through clothing, skin, flesh, most woods and some thin sheet metal. It will not go through concrete, thick metal more than one centimetre thick, or bone. Its maximum distance is six hundred meters with a very concentrated beam. The shotgun effect will work out to about one hundred metres. Be very careful with glass and mirrors because there is sometimes the energy beam can get redirected. As for the benefits of this weapon, it is silent, absolutely no noise, no rounds to carry (only batteries) and they are good for hundreds, even thousands of shots depending upon what you are doing with it. There is also no muzzle flash as with a conventional weapon," Brook finishes.

We spend some time on the range comparing this new weapon to older rifles and handguns. After a couple of hours we return to the main group for lunch and none of us can believe what the others are telling us. We hear stories of tiny drones that can blow up an entire bridge, four man tactical remote submarines, full body ballistic suits and the list goes on and on. The rest of that day we spend learning how to use a small remote controlled sub. I am like a kid in a video game. I simply can't believe this is real. These are things I had heard of but never imagined I would be using and be trained to use.

The next morning we are on a flight back to Trenton and I am still in awe at what I have seen. Johns and Caloway are both excited and a little bit nervous. "Man oh man, do we have a lot of shit to learn, eh," Caloway says. "Yeah but this is going to be a lot of fun," Johns interjects. "We just have to make sure we bring Sims up to speed when he gets here," I state. "Yeah, is he going to have to do that whole course over without us?" Johns asks me. "I was told he would do it with the group coming in next month," I say. "Do you think he will be ready to go by then?" Calloway asks. "If I know him he is probably ready to go now. Let's see if we can get him on a TUFF Pad." I reach up above my head and grab a TUFF Pad and find his number at the hospital and call it. Sims answers, "Hey asshole, how you doin'?" "Alright we are just on our way home and thought we should call and see how the leg is," I respond. "Actually, I ran on the treadmill today for the first time, it hurt but I did three kilometres," he states with a smile. "When are you getting out?" Calloway asks. "In two days they are going to ship me out, I should be ready for duty in two weeks," he states boldly.

We shoot the shit with Sims for a few more minutes and then each of us calls our wives and kids. Six hours later I am home and barbequing steaks on my pool deck.

"So how did it go?" my wife asks. "Actually, I think I like it. They tested the shit out of us but it was alright. We have a lot of new equipment to learn," I say with a smile. "Well you always did like playing with the new stuff, right?" she asks. "Yeah and this stuff is really new. No one else in the world has these things. It'll be fun," I state again with a smile.

We go in and eat supper with the kids and hang around by the pool. This summer is half over and the kids will be getting ready to go back to school soon. I am off for two more weeks before I go back again. We plan a camping trip to Algonquin Park and stay for three days until it rains. We get home and the sun comes out. It happens every time.

I stay fit by running and lifting weights three times a week and riding my bike with the kids every day. I go to a boxing class and a wrestling class once a week just to keep my fighting skills sharp. I don't know if I need it or not, I just like keeping fit. I don't know if I could lose any fitness even if I sat on the couch for two weeks. I think we all feel pretty invincible right now.

A couple of days later I get a call from Sims. "Hey how are you doin'?" he asks me as if I was the one that got shot. "I'm great, how about you?" I ask. "I've been at the weights and running a little, I still use a cane a little bit, but I am making leaps and bounds," he says confidently. "Hey, you want to come over for a beer or something?" I ask him. "Yeah sure, when?" he asks. "I don't know how about tomorrow?" I reply. "Yeah, I can drive now, what can I bring?" he asks. "Just Cindy, the kids will love to see you two. I'll get Johns and Calloway to come too," I say. "OK, I'll see you tomorrow then," he finishes. I hang up the phone and call Johns and Calloway and get them to bring their wives and girlfriends over for dinner. Calloway has a girlfriend that he never brings anywhere. I have started to think she is a myth. Johns and Sims are both married.

The next day everyone comes over for dinner and drinks. We swim and hang around out by the pool all day and into the evening. Sims walks around like he was never injured. He has a huge scar that is almost healed. Every time I look at him I almost cry. I still feel so bad for him getting shot. I guess this is a good thing, it will keep me sharp. I won't make the same mistake twice. Calloway hangs around with our kids just as he always does. He is just like them, playful and giddy. Calloway's girlfriend hangs around with all the wives and fits in as if she had always been here.

Later in the day we start talking about our new jobs. The wives listen intently wanting to know every detail in case there was something they had not heard yet. We tell Sims about the test we had to do. For us it really wasn't that hard and Sims will pass easily. We give him every detail so that when he does it he will know exactly what to do. As always after enough alcohol has been poured the war stories start to come out. The wives always pretend that they are not listening. I try to steer the conversation in a different direction which usually ends with someone telling me to shut up.

Around 2:30 am I finally go to bed and everyone decides to stay over. We have an extra bedroom downstairs and everyone else gets a couch. I am really too drunk to care. I fall into bed and don't hear anything until the next morning.

I awake to the smell of bacon and eggs. I drag myself out of bed and go to the washroom. I grab a glass in the kitchen and drink three glasses of water and then grab a bottle of Tylenol and take three. I am met with a chorus of good mornings. Of course, it's Calloway who is the first one up cooking breakfast. The kids are giving him orders and he is making them whatever they want. He is always the first one up, no matter where we go.

I head back to my bedroom and put on a t-shirt and shorts. I head down the hall and put on my running shoes and head out the door. I always try to run off my hangovers. Usually it works, it just depends upon how bad the injury is. After about five kilometres I head back feeling pretty good now. I stretch my legs out on the deck and head back in for some more water. As I am standing there drinking my wife eyes me. "So how are you now?" she asks.

"Better," I answer. I grab a plate of food and sit down.

Soon everyone is back in the kitchen. "So we are all going into the park to go for a walk downtown, are you in?" Calloway asks. "Sure, just let me get into the shower. Twenty minutes, OK?" I head down to my bedroom again and jump in the shower. I get dressed and we all head into town. We go for a walk down by the beach and have lunch in town. Everyone leaves after lunch and we head back home.

When I get back in I check my email and I have new orders to be back at the training facility in Texas in two days. The summer has really flown by. I tell my wife about my orders and she is OK with it. I was home for almost three weeks this time. My new orders say I will be gone for six days. This will be a breeze. I can do anything for six days. I email everyone else and they all have the same orders. Sims will go ahead of us to do the testing and evaluation phase before we get there.

Once again I met everyone in Trenton for the short plane trip to Texas. We land at 9:00 am and are ready to go by 10:00 am. Sims and four other new recruits did all of the testing before we got there. I always assumed that Sims would pass. Sims leg is completely healed now. You would never even believe that his leg was ever injured. There is hardly a scar and he runs as well as he ever did.

We get right down to the training as soon as we get there. This time it is all water training. We look as some new breathing apparatus and a couple of new eight man submarines, as well as, an assortment of new landing craft. The training goes well. We live for this shit. Everyone is focused and really eager to learn this new stuff. I am amazed at how much there is to learn and most of these things are new. I have never manned an eight man sub or any other sub for that matter.

We spent two days with the subs before we took them out. We all got to man the subs one at a time; everyone else was learning different types of breathing apparatus. I took the sub out first and I loved it. I drove it with one of the instructors around a small bay for about half an hour on the surface and then we dove down about 20 feet. It is a lot like driving a car. There is a steering wheel and an accelerator, and controls to dive or surface. I returned to the dock, got off and stood there amazed. I began to think of all the tactical things we could do with a piece of equipment like this. These subs have a range of 400

Rod Bergeron

kilometres and are dead silent. My turn was over and I was off to try some new types of breathing apparatus.

Our training went on like this until the end of the year. We had lots of new things to learn and new stuff to tryout. We usually did two workouts a day, an hour of running in the morning and weights at night. We always ran with a pack and a weapon. We always had two sessions of fight training a day. We were taught every possible type of fighting: wrestling, boxing, kick boxing, Jiu Jitsu and knife fighting. Not only did we get fit, we also got silent. Everything we did was as silent as possible. There were days that no one ever spoke a word except the trainers. I was as fit as I could be. We were all fit. We had become the most elite fighters ever created and soon we would be put to the test.

There were thirty of us now and more were being trained every day. The base in Texas remained our base and it continued to grow as the numbers of us continued to grow.

There were dangers everywhere. The Russians were threatening the Chinese over oil. The fight continued in Somalia. There are skirmishes all over Africa. Central

America was a mostly lawless society. Mexico was at war with most of the Central American Countries for their oil. Mexico is now completely run by warlords who make money from the drug trade. The whole world was coming apart at the seams and we were going to have to help put it back together.

Part 3

Mexico. A true shit hole of a country; a lawless society where anyone could be killed for looking in the wrong direction. A place full of killers and warlords who fight for a price and who murder for fun. Mexico is still part of the North American Alliance that has been in place since 2025. Mexico has become so much a lawless society there is no country in the world that will allow tourists to go there; no government will grant visas to go there. It is truly a place without law and order of any type. The government, including the President and all of the Senators, have been in exile in the United States for over two years. Without tourism Mexico has no economy at all. Mexico is now relying on its drug trade and the taking of hostages to make money. Only those that are connected to the warlords in some way have food to eat and money to spend. Everyone else in Mexico wants out or has taken on some extreme measures to survive. Until the warlords amassed a fortune and were able to buy any weapon they wanted, no one cared about Mexico. No one gave it a second thought. Then the warlords united and were able to buy a surprise from the Iranians. A surprise no one ever thought could happen, a surprise in the shape of a nuclear warhead.

The United Iranian States, U.I.S., are another group of true assholes. They have spit at every United Nations sanction for over a hundred years and have become the bully of the Middle East. The U.I.S. government will sell arms including nuclear weapons to anyone with money. Mexico has been in negotiations with U.I.S. for years but not until a week ago were they able to get a nuclear warhead. The Mexicans now need a launch vehicle to fire the warhead and there is information that they are now talking to the Chinese to acquire a missile.

I am just packing the last of my clothes and getting ready to head back home when a voice comes over the P.A. telling us to assemble in the main hanger. We all look at each other. I grab my note pad and a pen, shove them in my pocket and head up. When we get upstairs there are piles of equipment and weapons and people moving around like there is a problem.

We head over to the main meeting area where the General and some of his officers are having a conversation and there is obviously some planning going on. I look at my guys and they look at me. I have a feeling like something big has just happened. I see some maps up on the large screens and some weather reports on the board as well as some satellite imagery of what looks to be a harbour and an airfield. It looks like everything we would need for a mission. There are thick files that look like they have taken many months to put together. This does not look to me like a mission someone just threw together. My palms are sweaty and my mouth is dry. I am nervous and I am never nervous about a mission.

I must look nervous because Colonel Morton comes over and stands beside me. "You know what is going on here?" he asks. "Not a clue Colonel," I reply. "You look like you know something," is his reply. "I don't have a good feeling about this," I say. He looks at me and gives a little laugh. "You never struck me as a superstitious type, Zeke," he says. I think to myself that is the first time he has used my first name. I think for a second. "I'm not usually, this time something's different," I reply.

There are now the five original groups: two from Great

Britain, two from the United States and one from Canada. There are also four other partially trained groups. There is one from Great Britain, one from the United States, one from Australia and one from France. In total there are nine teams of four.

General Fitch comes to the front of the seating area. "Please gentlemen, come and have a seat," he asks. We all go over to the seating area and sit and wait for him to begin. "Gentlemen, we have a situation that is going to require your attention. There is a situation in Mexico that has escalated in the last several hours. This unit has been tasked to deal with it. The warlords that now run Mexico have united and have purchased a nuclear warhead from U.I.S. Mexico having a nuclear warhead is one problem. In the last several hours the Mexicans have also taken possession of an intercontinental ballistic missile or ICBM, from China. We have confirmed with satellite imaging that a Chinese sub unloaded an ICBM this afternoon. We are currently trying to ascertain the type of missile and its range. We have been tracking the warhead since its arrival in Mexico because it has a radiation signature. This radiation signature is not large so we believe it must be well shielded and should pose no threat to humans. We have its exact location and have uploaded it to your HUD. We continue to monitor the Chinese missile and have also uploaded its position to your HUD. That is the situation," he takes a breather. HUD stands for Heads Up Display. The HUD allows the user to see what is happening around himself as well as access information that is required at a specific time, such as weather reports of tactical information.

"Your mission is two-fold. First, get possession of the warhead and safely move it out of Mexico and secondly destroy the missile. We will execute this mission in four phases. One group will land in the docklands near the missile. Insertion of this team will be by ten man sub. A second group will land near the main airport where the warhead is, by air drop from a CF23. A third group will secure an area north of the airport to be used as an extraction area; this group will also be used as a reserve force and will also go in by CF23," the general moves over to the maps.

"There is 1.5 kilometres between the docklands and the

airport. After the first group has set the charges they will move to a safe area and detonate. This first group should then move to the extraction point at the airport. The second group will acquire the warhead at the airport by any means necessary and move it to the extraction point. Group one and two should link up with group three in the safe area for extraction. There will be Scorpion helicopters on standby for extraction. The Scorpions will originate from an aircraft carrier in the Gulf of Mexico. There will also be an AWACS on site for surveillance as well as drones." He takes another breather and walks towards us. "All teams will depart for the aircraft carrier Vendome in thirty minutes. Are there any questions?" he asks.

I raise my hand first; the General points to me. "Sir which groups will get which assignments?" I ask. "This is a group of free thinking highly trained people, I'll let you decide," he states. I look around for someone to start talking and no one does. "I think my group and Colonel Morton's group should go in on the ten man sub. We have logged the most hours on it so far," I suggest. "I would agree," says Colonel Morton. "I agree, you will also have a sub mariner to drive for you and return the sub to the carrier Vendome," he states flatly. "Who wants the airport assignments?" the general asks. I stop listening. I just volunteered to take a sub to a hostile country and blow up a missile and carry a nuclear warhead out of the country. What the fuck is wrong with me? My guys sit stoned face and listen to the rest of the conversation. The general dismisses us and we head off to our quarters.

We get on the elevator and head down to the sixth floor. "Guys, weapons and equipment check in ten minutes," I say to them. They all nod. I walk off the elevator and down the hall, my mind drifts off. I was to be half way home by now. I need to send a message to my wife. I go to the computer at my desk and type a quick email telling her I am going on some more training and that I will be home in two days. That was my code to my wife that I was safe and will be home soon.

I go over and get my weapons bag out of my locker and check it out. Everything is where it should be. I change into my clean black combat shirt and pants. I pack my SHIT suit carefully in my duffle bag. I change my socks and tie my boots like they may not be off for a while. I tuck a knife into each boot and put my service knife on my belt on my right hip. I put my C.E.W.H.G., (Concentrated Energy Weapon Hand Gun), on the belt on my left hip. I check my pack. I have my SHIT suit which is a new type of stealthy technology we have been training to use, more about that later. I have my gloves, rope, communications gear, extra batteries for my SHIT suit and weapon. I grab my helmet. I'm ready to go. I move over to where my guys are and we go through our weapons check. I really don't have to do this, it's routine and if my guys don't know basic shit like this they are in the wrong place. Everyone has everything and is ready.

The equipment is all being loaded onto the Scorpions. We get on the Scorpions and buckle up. I close the door and grab one of the TUFF pads. I type in my security code. I check the mission details and commit them to memory. Everyone else is doing their own thing, looking out the window, playing with their knives and in general, fucking around.

We are at the carrier in twenty minutes. The sun is just starting to set and the sky is a brilliant red.

Once the Scorpion is down I pull the door open and jump out. We grab our bags and are quickly directed by the carrier staff over to the side where we all meet in the large aircraft elevator. I go over to the other teams and wish them luck and we all joke and laugh. There is always a joke about someone's mother. All of the teams get off at the first lower deck except for Colonel Morton's team and mine. We go down to the very bottom where the ten man subs are. "Holy fuck where are we going to?" says Sims. "Way down into the belly of the beast," replies the man running the controls of this giant elevator. "Where you boys off to?" he asks with a deep southern accent. "We're going straight to hell my lad, otherwise known as Mexico," says Colonel Morton. "Fuck you guys are either really brave or really fuckin' stupid," he says as we reach the bottom. "This is your stop, good luck," he finishes.

We all get off into a huge well lit area. There are lots of people waiting for us. "Good day gentleman, I am Commander Brody, I am tasked with getting you to your destination safely today," he says very politely. "I understand you have all had some training in the ten man subs, have any of you ever been on an aircraft carrier

before?" he asks. We all shake our heads no. "Well now
you have. We have about an hour before we are to leave so
I have arranged some food in our mess. I'll take you there
now," he leads us off down a narrow corridor and through
a couple of hatches.

We all file into the mess and there is all kinds of food. I
grab a blueberry muffin and a carton of milk. The rest of
my guys grab full meals, of course. These fuckers would
eat anything that's not tied down. I once saw the three of
them eat a whole fuckin' turkey in three minutes, mashed
potatoes, peas, gravy and all. You would think that all that
food would slow them down, but not these vultures.

There is the usual banter back and forth; the Canadians
screwing with the British and the British just laughing at
the whole affair. I sit back and eat my muffin and drink
my milk; I know that soon enough all the laughter and
silliness will have to stop. Sims sits across from me with
a plate of spaghetti that would choke a dinosaur and five
slices of garlic bread. Calloway has about the same
amount of spaghetti, but he also has three of the biggest
meatballs I have ever seen. Johns sits at the table across

from me with two pork chops and a mountain of potatoes. I just shake my head. Then I see that all of the Colonel's guys have about the same amount of food.

Commander Brody comes over and sits with my guys and I. "Do you think it would be alright to start the briefing soon," he asks. I look at him and give him a nod. My guys all stop and give him a smile and a nod. He stands back up and gives us a little smile. He walks up to the front of the room and the group comes to a hush quickly.

Commander Brody introduces himself once again and welcomes everyone on board the Aircraft Carrier Vendome. He asks us if we all have teams selected and the numbers on each team. He does a safety briefing about the ten men subs and everyone pays close attention to him. I watch my guys and keep an eye on Colonel Morton and his men because I know that we are going to be working together. He turns the men's attention back to their respected leaders and reminds us that we have 30 minutes.

"OK guys suit up and we will do an equipment check in

ten minutes," I tell my guys with some authority. They all quickly scarf back the rest of their food. We shake Commander Brody's hand and leave to suit up. We are lead down a long hallway to a staging area to get dressed.

Our suits are state of the art in warfare equipment. Known as stealth, high impact, integrated, thermal blocking suits or SHIT suits as the troops have come to know them. These suits provide the wearer a completely stealthy appearance. The suit is made of thousands of tiny cameras and projection screens. Everything in the wearer's vicinity is constantly photographed and then projected onto the tiny projection screens to make the wearer almost invisible. The early generations of these suits would only allow the wearer to move at a slow walking pace. This newer generation allows the wearer to run and still remain invisible. The one drawback is that it doesn't work in the rain. If it gets wet, it is fucked. The cameras and the projector screens just won't project when they are wet.

The suit will also deflect most bullets but not sniper rounds or any large caliber rounds like 50 caliber. Kevlar vests are no longer worn by any of us. The suit is also knife proof. The suit is fully integrated into the electronic battlefield system. The suit allows commanders to monitor each soldier's heart rate, breathing and other medical information. If a soldier becomes injured for any reason his situation can be assessed by a doctor in headquarters and information about how to treat each soldier is immediately sent to others in the area. The helmets are usually referred to as HUD's. HUD stands for "heads up display". The HUD gives the soldier all the information one could possibly ever want. There are some simple uses for the HUD. It gives direction traveled, distance to a target and maps of the area much like any GPS. The visor can turn night into day when in night vision mode. There is barely any difference between daylight and night. The HUD can also relay information about how to fix a medical situation for any member. The HUD can also deliver information about how to fix a vehicle.

The suits also diminish a soldier's heat signature to that of a small mouse. There are no weapons able to pick up a soldiers heat signature while wearing a SHIT suit. The heat is diffused by the suit so much that there are times you freeze your ass off. There is a heat source that is battery operated by a small lithium battery pack that is contained on the soldiers back.

There are also pockets for extra batteries for the weapons systems and the suit itself as well as knives, grenades and other equipment. On the back there is a two litre camel back for water and a small pouch for some quick energy food. I usually fill mine with chocolate bars and energy bars. I also carry a large knife on my side and a boot knife in each boot. I have two throwing stars on my belt buckle and a collapsible baton next to my side arm. I also carry thirty feet of rope on my back.

Most of us carry the same equipment. Each of us has the opportunity to bring whatever we want as long as the commanding officer OKs it. There are strict rules on what we cannot bring. There are no family pictures of any kind allowed, ever. Rings or other jewellery are never allowed. No identification of any type, no dog tags, driver's licence, not even a library card. We don't give the enemy anything to use against us if we are ever captured. We certainly don't want them to ever trace anything back to find our families.

Johns is the point man and carries a new version of the
high energy weapon; a rifle-shotgun combination as well
as his medical equipment. Terry Sims carries a sniper rifle
version of the high energy weapon, several charges of C4
or other types of explosives. Chris Calloway also carries a
rifle-shotgun combination like Johns, a small collapsible
satellite antenna and a tiny little communication centre.
The first time I saw the communications centre I thought it
was a box of candy. It's tiny but it can connect to a
satellite in seconds.

After dressing, some people have their own little rituals,
some people pray, some meditate, some tell jokes. I just
sit and go over the plan. I go over it until it is cemented
into my mind. I go over it until it makes me sick. I plan
for every possible scenario. I plan for snipers. I plan for
counter attacks. I plan for extractions in different places.
I plan for fucking everything. So far it has saved my skin
and the ass of all of my guys. Everyone knows that I am
an obsessive planner. They also know when shit goes bad
I probably have a way out.

Colonel Morton stands at the front and asks to do an equipment check. We go over weapons and batteries. We do a battery check for the suits. Next we check the stealth operation. As I look across the room there is not a person to be seen. Everyone melts into the walls of the room. All that can be seen is white walls with a red strip all the way around the room. "That is so fucking cool," a lone voice says from the rear. It is cool. It's a little frightening also. We all turn off the stealth one after the other and all look a little surprised when we see where everyone is. We finish with a check of our HUD's and communications.

Commander Brody comes to the door and sticks his head in. He nods. That tells us it's time to go. We all stand and follow him down the hall to a giant metal door. Two sailors push the door open and we all walk in. There is a giant room and two, ten man subs floating in water. There is a catwalk overhead that leads to the doors on the top of the subs. There is light coming from inside the water and there are a couple of divers in the water. The floor is actually metal grates that have a tinny echoing sound as we walk across. The sound of many boots all walking on the metal grates at the same time echoes through the large room. We walk towards the subs and Commander Brody yells to us, "Best of luck." I give him thumbs up. He nods back. I walk across the cat walk and step to the door. I take a quick look down and start down the ladder. The inside of the sub is well lit and I take a seat. The sub commander comes towards us and smiles, "Ready gentleman?" he asks. I look at him and smile and give him thumbs up. The rest of the teams follow me down into the sub.

Everyone around me is talking and laughing and I barely know they are there. I can see them, I can feel them, but for now I am happy just living in my head. I look at my watch, its 2000 hours. It has only been three hours since we first got told of this mission. Three hours to prepare and be on route to a mission. No other group in the world could do this in that amount of time. I look up and grab a TUFF pad from the rack near the roof. I enter my identification number and upload the mission. I look at the maps and go over the plan again. I look at all of the code words and burn them into my mind. Several others around me stop the laughing and get serious about what we are about to do. I see a lot of other TUFF pads being pulled down and looked at. I look at my GPS on my watch and make sure it is the same coordinates as the TUFF pad. They are all the same.

I study the maps and learn all of the entrances and exits for the building we are going into. There are two entrances that are close to the dock where we will be surfacing. My head starts to sweat under my helmet. I take it off and wipe my head. It is starting to get warm inside the sub. Colonel Morton sits across from me and he points to his ear and then points to me. That is the signal for someone is trying to talk to you. I wipe my bristly short haired head with my hand one more time and put my helmet back on. I immediately hear a voice in my ear. "Lieutenant Heron are you there?" a voice asks. "This is Heron, over," I say. "This is AWACS Commander to all call signs please confirm call signs," the Commander asks. The airborne groups go first. First the group going to the airport, then the group going as the reserve force then Colonel Morton and I'm last. I am call sign Red. I am Red one, Johns is Red two, Sims is Red three and Calloway is Red four. Colonel Morton is Blue One.

Immediately the call signs are all uploaded to our HUD and we can see each call sign's position on a map. All we have to do is look at a particular call sign and look to the left of it where is says "map" and a map will pop up. All of this happens while I can still see through the visor and I can hear the other call signs still talking in my ear piece. I can turn the volume up or down simply by saying into my mic, "volume down." The HUD can understand hundreds of voice commands and an endless amount of eye movements.

I push my visor up and out of the way. I can see on the TUFF Pad in front of me that we are a long way off and our ETA (estimated time of arrival) is 2 hours. The first reserve units are only an hour out from their staging point and the airport team is one hour and thirty minutes away from their drop zone. The reserve units will stay hidden until needed and will be in place long before the attacking forces begin their assaults. I think to myself, "two more hours in this tin can". It is pretty comfortable, but really getting warm and the air is thick. The seats are nicely padded and there is plenty of room to move so that we are not on top of each other. It is starting to get warmer, but a fan comes on every couple of minutes to cool things off.

I hear in my earpiece that the hatches are closing and there is a strange grinding noise. The sub starts to move a little to the left and then to the right. Then I hear in my earpiece, "go for docking release". We are being let go, away from the carrier and off into the ocean. We begin to point down a little and then begin to pick up speed. There is a hum to the motors and a slight vibration in the floor. I grab onto the seat between my legs and can feel my palms sweaty on the vinyl seat. I look across and see concerned faces on almost everyone. Then all at once everyone starts to lighten up. Sims says, "This is actually kind of cool." "That's just because Johns isn't driving. Remember what he did in the bay?" I say over the mic. "Yeah when he had us almost upside down," Calloway says. Everyone laughs, even Johns. "Wait what was that?" a far off voice asks. It's one of the guys in a plane high above us asking for details about the incident. The comic relief is always good to keep everyone awake and on task.

I close my eyes and allow my mind to wander. I think of

home and my family. I allow it to go on for some time as I wonder what they are doing and where they are. I dream of the summer nights and watching the stars with my kids and thinking about all of the wonderful adventures they will have in their lives. All the places in the stars they may someday get to visit and all of the wonderful things to discover. I dream of their future and the future of all of the world's children and a world without war, a world of peace and happiness for all of the world's children. My mind wanders and I let it. Time drifts by and I float on its many coloured waves. I am at peace.

With some degree of control I bring myself back to the present. Gently, I bring myself back. I listen before I open my eyes. There is hardly a sound. I can hear myself breathing. Then there is a slight crackle in my earpiece and then a far off voice asking for some direction. Mostly what I hear around me is my own breath. I listen. The hum of the engines vibrates under my feet. The humming is soothing and tranquil. I realize the depth of what I am about to do. I understand the risk. I understand who we are and what we have to do. My eyes are open, but are they?

I open my eyes and look at my HUD. I click on maps and then click on current location. I see we are still in the Gulf of Mexico and we are twenty nine minutes from the destination. There is some radio traffic between the AWACS Commander and the first troops jumping into the night sky. It's 2200 hours and everyone is starting to get a little edgy. I push my visor up and look down the row of seats. There are a couple of guys playing cards. I really don't give a shit what game they are playing, but they look like they are having a great time of it. There are a couple of other guys who are playing games on the TUFF Pads. Johns is shaking the shit out of his TUFF Pad like it owes him money or something. I let them play. Soon enough we will have to get serious. I try to check my email but the AWACS must be jamming all of the satellite signals. I hear some more chatter about the troops that have now landed at the air field. All of the reserve forces are now on the ground and are securing their perimeter. Everyone else hears the radio chatter and has set down their TUFF Pads and stopped playing cards.

The sub commander comes on the radio. "Gentleman, we are fifteen minutes out. We are initiating blackout so that your eyes can adjust to your night vision. All Copy?" he asks. When he says, "All Copy," he is asking if we all understand or if we all agree. "Blue leader, copy," says Colonel Morton. "Red leader copy," I respond quickly. I think to myself this is the first time I haven't had to ask to go to blackout. Most load masters in plane and crew chiefs on ships don't usually know we want to go to blackout so our eyes can adjust. This guy knows his shit. As the lights go out our night vision kicks in right away. Everyone has a strobe light that comes on when the night vision gear is functioning. You cannot see it with the naked eye but when the AWACS plane looks down on us they can identify us by the strobe light on the back of our helmet.

The lights go out. I pull my visor down and my HUD comes on. My night visor comes on and everything goes an eerie shade of green. There is more radio chatter. The airport assault group has all landed safely and has set up a secure perimeter. There is more radio chatter about our distance and time to target. The AWACS Commander tells them to wait for further instructions. I click on my map and I see we are only a two minutes away from the landing site. Our landing point is a dock that is about two hundred metres away from the building we are to assault.

"AWACS Command to Blue and Red leaders, radio check over," he asks coolly. "Blue leader copy," says Colonel Morton. "Red leader copy," I repeat. "We are updating satellite and radar images to your HUD now. There are five targets on the exterior, three on the ground and two on the roof, as well as ten inside. There are no friendlies in this area. All weapons are cleared to go hot," he says confidently. "Blue leader copy," says Colonel Morton. "Red leader copy," I repeat.

"One minute to target," says the sub commander. My breath quickens. My palms are sweaty. My heart beats hard in my chest. "You are clear to go to stealth," says the AWACS Commander. I click on my stealth and I can see my own strobe light in my HUD as well as all the other strobe lights around me. "Ok let's keep our shit tight out there tonight, let's go," I stand up. I sling my rifle on my back. I pull my black gloves out of my pocket and put them on. "We are breaking the surface. Hatches are releasing. We are in place. Clear for exit," says the sub commander.

As the hatch opens I tap the sub commander on the shoulder as if to say thanks. He gives me a nod. I decide to go first. I can hear the splashing of the waves before I am even starting up the ladder. I climb up. As I get to the top I see that there's no moonlight and only three overhead street lights illuminating the dock. I move up to the top and stand on the outside of the sub. I reach over and grab the ladder on the dock and slowly make my way to the top of it. I look down to see my guys right behind me. I clear the ladder and kneel down. Very quickly all eight of us are at the top.

Completely concealed by our stealth suits we walk slowly towards the three men on the ground level. Colonel Morton's team takes the two on the right and Johns moves over to the one nearest us. He turns on his handgun and shoots the man in the back of the head. The man falls forward and Sims and Calloway catch him before he hits the ground. They drag him around the corner and put him behind a dumpster. As they remove him Colonel Morton comes on the radio. "Blue leader, targets one and two neutralized," he says calmly. "Red leader, target three neutralized," I reply. "Blue leader, Blue two and Blue three moving to neutralize targets on roof," says Colonel Morton. "Red leader, holding position," I say. About a minute has passed since I last heard from Colonel Morton and I can see in my HUD that his two men have moved to the roof. They are right up to the two men on the roof. Blue two and Blue three move over to their targets and the men fall dead. "Blue two, both roof targets neutralized," he states flatly. "Blue two to all call signs there is a roof hatch. We can see targets. Permission to neutralize," he asks. "Blue leader, NO! Blue two, get back down here!" he orders.

About thirty seconds later the men are back down and with the Colonel. I crouch down and walk quietly past a lighted window unseen because of my stealth. The area is paved and covered with pebbles. There is no moonlight and it is very cloudy and dark. I can hear some chatter inside. Men laugh. I continue to walk to the east side of the building. I can see in my HUD that my guys are right behind me. I feel a hand on my shoulder. It's Johns. He stops me and takes the point position. "Red leader, we are entering the east side of the building. Let's do this quietly," I plead. "Blue leader, we are going in the west side," he states. As I enter I see this is a large open, well lit warehouse. The Chinese missile is in the middle of the area. There are two men sleeping on a couch near the missile and four playing cards. There is one man talking on the phone near what looks like a communications centre and one moving towards a washroom. I look at my HUD to see where the other two men are. They are in a small room behind the washroom it looks like they are also sleeping. On my HUD they are not moving. "Red leader, we are going to take the comms man, the two sleepers by the missile and the card players," I tell Colonel Morton. "Blue leader, copy that. We have the rest," he says.

"Red leader, Johns and Sims take the four card players. Calloway takes the two sleepers by the missile. I am taking the comms man. Colonel let me know when you are in place," I ask. A few seconds go by but they feel like hours. I move to within three feet of my target. I look in my HUD and see everyone move into place. "Blue leader, Blue team is in position," he states. I look around at my guys and see everyone is in place. "Red leader, Red team is in place. You call it Colonel," I ask him to say when. I pull my pistol out and turn it on. I am one foot away from the back of this man's head. "Blue leader, NOW!" he calls. I pull the trigger and the heavy set man falls to the desk in front of him and slumps over it. Within a second, ten men fall dead to the floor without a sound from any of us. I hang up the phone he was using. "Red leader to AWACS Command did you monitor that call," I ask. "AWACS Command, he was unable to make an outgoing call. We were blocking all of their communications. There is a vehicle moving towards your location. It has three men on board. Let's wait and see where they go," the AWACS Commander suggests.

"Red leader, Johns and Calloway to the door. Get eyes on the vehicle. Sims set your charges on that missile," I order. Colonel Morton orders his explosives expert to set his charges also. Their blurred images match the background almost exactly. All I can really see of them is a vague outline. But that is all I can see of any of us unless I am looking at the HUD. They quickly move into place. The charges of C4 become visible as they place them because they are no longer being concealed by the stealth. The British explosives expert also sets his C4 charges.

I look at my HUD to see Johns is kneeling and Calloway is standing right behind him at the doorway in the middle of the building. Both have their rifles up at the ready. "AWACS Command the vehicle is almost there. You should have a visual now. We may have another problem," he suggests. "Red two, we have a visual on the vehicle. There are three men, all armed. The vehicle is a large troop transport," Johns says. "Red Leader, let them all the way into the building and then take them," I order.

The AWACS Commander interrupts our conversation. "AWACS Command, we have a problem. It is starting to rain. Your stealth suits will be minimized," he says in a hurry. "Red leader, AWACS Command that may not be a problem. We are going to take this vehicle," I say. "Blue leader, I agree let's take these three and get the hell out of here," Colonel Morton says. "AWACS Command, to Blue and Red leaders, confirm that the C4 charges are set," he asks. "Blue leader, charges are set," Colonel

Morton says. "Red leader, charges are set," I say. I look and see that there is C4 all over the missile, about every metre along the side and four charges on the nose cone. This missile is a lot larger than I had expected. It is ten metres long and over a metre in diameter. It is mostly silver except for the four fins on the back, they are red. It sits length wise on four large metal supports. It looks ominous. Its warhead is Biterol, which is a dangerous explosive and packs a punch at least four times that of C4. Biterol can get hot enough to melt concrete.

The three men with the truck are now out and are calling names of the men to be on guard duty. They get no answer. They look nervous. They have their rifles at the ready and they move towards the door. They spread out and look right at Johns but don't see him. They keep moving ahead slowly and cautiously. They stop. They try to look past the door. They start to back up. More quickly they back up. "Take them now," I order. Three shots are fired and not a sound is made. All three men fall dead. "Red leader, get them in here now," I plead. Several men go out and drag the dead men into the building and drop them unceremoniously on the floor.

They are regular army just like the other men in the building. All have Mexican Army uniforms. "Red leader to Blue leader, can you make your way over here?" I ask. The rain comes down harder now. "Blue leader, where are you Red leader?" Colonel Morton asks. "Red leader, near the front entrance," I reply. Colonel Morton comes around the corner and sees me. I point to one of the dead men. I reach up and turn my mic off and he does the same. "Is this right? I thought these guys were a bunch of terrorist?" I ask. "Me too, these guys all have the same weapons, the same uniforms, what's up?" he adds. "If these guys don't show back up someone is going to come looking for them," I say. "Let's just blow this fucker up and get the fuck out of here," the Colonel replies.

The Colonel and I both turn our mics back on. "Blue leader to AWACS command, do the other teams have the package yet?" he asks if the warhead has been found. "AWACS command, the package is in hand. That team is awaiting your arrival," the Commander says. "Red leader to AWACS command, these men are all regular army. There must be a mistake in the intelligence," I suggest. "We will have a look at the video from your cameras later.

Can you take the vehicle?" he asks. All of our movements are recorded from a tiny camera in our helmets so that we can learn from our mistakes and possibly gain more intelligence later.

The Colonel orders two of his men to go and have a look at the vehicle. As they move out into the rain their stealth begins to diminish within a couple of seconds they are fully visible. "Red leader to Red team, turn off your stealth. We'll save it for later," I say. The Colonel orders the same. The two men in the vehicle give us the thumbs up and motion us to come out and we all pile in. The explosives guys are both together near the back gate. "AWACS command to Red and Blue leaders, you must be at least one kilometre away before you detonate. We will monitor. We are uploading the maps to the HUD now," he says. We get the directions to the airport and the driver takes off. I am already soaked all the way to the skin.

There is a lot of radio traffic and I can only make out part of it. Someone is under fire. That is not good. We may have been found out. "Blue leader to AWACS command, who is under fire?" he pleads. There is no answer. He tries again. "Blue leader to AWACS command, who is under fire?" he pleads desperately. "FUCK!" he cries out. "Blue leader to Red leader try to raise AWACS command," he begs. "Red leader to AWACS command, come in," I ask. Nothing. I try again. Nothing. I look at the Colonel and shake my head. He turns his mic off. "Let's try and get someone else," he says and turns his mic back on. I look at my HUD. We still have the directions to the airport and we are now half a kilometre from the missile. We are about half a kilometre away from being able to detonate the explosives. I turn my mic off. "Colonel lets blow the missile. Let's finish one objective and then worry about saving our asses," I yell. He nods yes. I look at my HUD. Two hundred metres to the detonation point. The Colonel gets his driver to pull over. "Stop here," he orders.

He turns his mic off. "Can we get a visual from here?" he asks me. "I think so," I say. I look back in the area of the docklands. The rain pours down on me. "Blow it, I'll make sure I get it on my helmet cam," I say. The two explosives guys take out their detonators and turn them on and press a large red button on top. The next instant a huge explosion can be heard and a large flash of light can be seen. I make sure I get it all on my helmet cam. "Someone knows we are here for fuckin' sure now," I say. "Let's go," the Colonel orders quickly.

We take off in a hurry. A small car passes us going the other way on the wet street. Our driver increases his speed dramatically. Then another car passes us. There is a huge flame ahead of us. Something is definitely on fire. Smoke is rising in the sky. I can smell the acrid smoke.

"Blue leader to any call signs, come in any call signs," he pleads. "Green leader, I hear you Blue Leader," another British voice says. It's the other British team. " Orange leader, I got you too Blue leader," the one American team leader announces. "White leader, we're here too Colonel," the other American team leader replies. "Green leader, what happened to AWACS command?" he asks. "Blue leader, we lost them too," says the Colonel. "Blue leader, OK airport team get ready to move in five," he orders. "Green leader copy that," he agrees. The Colonel turns off his mic again. "Let's assume that the extraction point is still at the same place," he states flatly. I nod. A round hits the truck. Then another. Then several more. I raise my riffle to fire back. I can't see anything for all of the smoke coming down the street. More rounds hit us. Not having any intell from the AWACS sucks. We fire at the roof tops as we go by.

The Colonel is to my right trying to get his mic straightened out in front of his mouth. He grabs his throat. Blood splatters all over me. He looks at me for help. He falls. I grab him and ease him to the floor of the truck. I grab his wound right at the base of his neck and put pressure on it. The Colonel got hit in one of the only unprotected parts on the whole suit. He stares at me as if begging to live. A medic pushes me to the side and cuts open his shirt at the neck. The bullet hole pours bright red blood shooting from the wound. "Sit him up!" says the medic frantically. The bullets still rain down on us. "Two minutes to the airport!" the driver screams as loud as he can.

SMASH. A truck drives right into the side of us. Men fly everywhere. The Colonel lands right on top of me. Men yell and moan in pain. The bullets still rain down on us.

"FUCK!" I yell. I push the Colonel off me. I grab my rifle and his and sling them over my back. "Come on Colonel we got to get the fuck out of here!" I scream to him. I grab him by the arm and pull him up to his feet. I bend over and sling him over my back. A round hits me right in my calf and bounces right off. I run to a nearby doorway. I move into the building and set the Colonel down on a sofa and run back to the door. There are men right behind me carrying other wounded. The medic rushes over to the Colonel and is working on him. I see there are others still trying to get out of the truck. I run back out to see the driver and the other man in the front are dead. There is a man trapped under the side of the truck trying to pull himself out. Several of us rush to him and we lift the truck up just enough to pull him free. He is the last man. His leg is badly bruised, but not broken. He winces in pain, but does not scream, not even a tear. I grab two rifles left in the melee and get shot in the back of the leg by another bullet for my trouble. It stings, but I run.

"Fuck me," I say as I get back in the door. "Snipers get as high up as you can. Get rid of whoever the fuck is shooting at us. GO!" I demand. "Medic, give me a report!" I yell as I shoot two men crossing the street towards us. Bullets are hitting hard all around us. It is very dark out and the rain continues to pound down. The streets are a river of mud. "Someone get on these fuckin' front windows," I call. "Medic how bout it?" I ask Johns again. "We have two dead and one wounded," the medic calls. "How is the Colonel?" I ask. "He is losing a lot of blood, but I have an IV set up and he is still with us," he calls back.

There are only six of us now and the Colonel is injured very badly. "Red leader to all call signs we are going to need a little help here," I beg. "Green leader, what is your situation Red leader?" he asks. "We are in a first floor home about a click from the airport. We have two dead and one wounded. Our transport is destroyed. We are going to need some help getting out of here," I ask. "I have your position on my HUD. We will have to get the reserve forces over here now. Stay put I'll get back to you," he states. "Red leader, copy that," I say.

I hear a lot of chatter between the reserve forces and the

Green leader. I hear another voice trying to cut in on our frequency. I think that maybe it is AWACS command but I can't be sure. The gunfire coming in our direction has slowed down a lot. The snipers must be doing their job. I see on my HUD a sniper on the roof looking east and another facing west, both are lying down. "Red three to Red leader, we are beating them back," Sims says. "Great job guys keep it up. Can anyone see the airport?" I ask. "Red three to Red leader, I am on the roof and I can see the airport control tower from here. It is straight down the road in front of us," he states. "Red leader, try to keep that road open Red three," I ask.

"Green leader to Red leader, come in," he asks. "Red leader send over," I ask for his reply. "Green leader, we have the reserve forces coming to collect the package and return it to the extraction point. We also have a vehicle and will shortly be on our way to pick you up. Can you hold on?" he asks. "Red leader, do I have a fucking choice? Get here as soon as you can," I say. "Green leader, we will get to you just hold on," he asks. "Red leader, copy that. Do you still have us on your HUD?" I ask. "Green leader, I still have your position. The vehicle is just coming to pick us up now. Hold on," he begs. On my HUD I can see six men get into a truck and begin to drive towards us. What and the hell has happened to AWACS? Why can't we contact them? I decided to try again.

"Red leader to AWACS command, come in AWACS," I ask. There is no reply, but there is a lot of static. "Red leader to AWACS command, we cannot hear you. Please try to adjust your signal," I ask again. There is static again, but there are some broken words also. I am squatting down just inside the door and to the left. I am leaning against someone's kitchen wall. I can see right down the street to our front. Beside me there is a sink full of dirty dishes and a frying pan on the floor. I look behind me to make sure no one else is in the building. There is no one home here. A bullet hits the wall right beside me. I change views on my HUD and see one of our snipers turn and fire in that direction. Someone definitely knows we are here and I imagine they are not too pleased about us blowing up their missile. Every minute we sit here we become more of a target.

The rain has started to lighten up and the streets are still dark. I can smell the rain as it mixes with the mud on the street. I grab the hose from my camel back and take a drink for the first time in a long while. I am hungry, but have no time to think about that right now. "Red three to Red leader," Sims calls. "Red leader, go Red three," I reply. There is a truck moving in our direction from the airport. It could be our guys," he states. "Red leader, stay frosty everyone. Remember to keep that road clear if we can," I try to reassure them. I can hear a truck now. It seems to be a long way off. The rain drowns out the engine noise.

"Green leader to Red leader, we are approaching you now. We are about three hundred metres out," he says. Just as the words come out of his mouth rifle fire begins in their direction. The rounds are large probably fifty caliber. I can hear some of the rounds hitting metal and think they are hitting the truck. Immediately the snipers fire back from the roof; soon after I hear yelling and screaming coming from the truck. I can see our guys on my HUD, but none of the enemy. I think to myself AWACS must still be down, we could really use them right now.

I peer down the darkened road in front of us and I can see movement. Men are crossing the road in the direction of the truck. I raise my rifle and fire. I fire again at the men crossing the road and hit several of them. No more men cross the road. Several of the men on the road are only injured and I shoot their rescuers as they try to pull them to safety. I can hear calls for help and screams of pain and I watch closely to make sure no one else is crossing.

I look to my HUD again. I can see the snipers turn and I assume they fire back. Fuck, I don't like this. In the past I could hear the snipers fire back at the enemy. Now with these new weapons there is no noise to tell where anyone is. I can hear bullets coming at us hitting metal and ricochets, the noise is constant. The rain has lightened up considerably now. There are still a few drops in the puddles just outside the door. I can hear the truck better now. "Green leader to Red leader, we are just about there. How long will it take you to evacuate?" he asks. "Red leader, only a couple of seconds. You will have to provide us some cover fire," I reply. "Green leader, you got it," is his reply. I hear the truck pulling up out front. There is almost no rifle fire coming at us now. I guess the snipers have got their targets. "Red leader to Green leader, I want those dead men out of that truck. We are not leaving them here," I plead. "Green leader, copy that Red leader," he says. I know he won't want to leave these men behind especially because they are British like him. No one should ever be left behind. Never.

"This is AWACS command, we are back online. What is the current situation?" he asks. "Thank fuck," I say to myself. "Red leader, we have two dead and one wounded from the Blue team. Green team is here to assist us. Can you give us any enemy positions?" I beg. The Green team piles out of the truck and rush over to the dead men. One is removed quickly and thrown over someone's back and taken to the truck. The second is wedged in against the door. "Red leader to snipers, cover those men out front," I command. "Red leader to medic, get the Colonel ready to move," I order. I rush out to help pry open the door. Four of us grab on and pull the door out of the thick mud. Two men grab the dead man and rush him to the truck. His lifeless body sways and his head drops back, low to the ground and brushes into the mud. The mud is slippery and we all slide on it.

Rod Bergeron

Our snipers on the roof top are still firing rapidly trying to suppress the enemy. From the ground we continue to fire back at the black faceless silhouettes trying to kill us. We never see any faces or hear any moans, but we are sure we got them because they no longer fire back.

I can hear the AWACS Commander talking with some of the other teams. He now knows that we have destroyed the missile and the warhead is with the reserve forces awaiting extraction at the north end of the airport. The reserve forces have come under heavy fire and the two American teams have moved out to try and track down the enemy.

"Red leader to snipers, continue to suppress the enemy fire. Medic, move the injured out to the truck. Everyone get ready to move," I command. The enemy fire comes in hard on us now. They must see that we are getting ready to move. The snipers fire quickly. "Red leader to AWACS command we need some intell, NOW!" I beg. "AWACS command to all call signs uploading enemy positions to your HUD now," he says confidently.

"Red two to Red leader, the two of us can cover your route out. Can you get a Scorpion to pick us up here?" Sims asks. He and the Blue team's sniper are asking to be left behind so that they may cover us until we get back to the airport. It's a great suggestion, but I really do not feel good about leaving two men behind to fend for themselves. They could be overrun by the enemy easily if not extracted in time. "Red leader to AWACS Command, did you copy last? Is that a possibility?" I ask. Rounds are hitting right beside the door of the truck I am leaning against. The medic has the Colonel out to the truck and they have slid him under a long metal seat at the back of the truck. "AWACS command, we copy last and are redirecting Scorpion helicopters now. Get that truck and you're wounded out now. I will command the snipers from here," he suggests. "Red leader, I copy that. Calloway you stay with them and cover their backs. We are moving now," I command.

"Red four, understood. Holding position," Calloway says as if he is staying for a birthday party. The truck driver is already in reverse and has got us turned around. He floors it and drives right over a curb and knocks over anything in his path. I can hear the Scorpion helicopters now. There sounds like lots of them. I see two of them pass right over us and then hover over the street. There MINI guns open up and a rain of bullets fly from them. The truck driver speeds up even more. I can hear the AWACS Commander talking to the guys we left behind. We smash through a chain link fence that surrounds the airport. No gate or entrance he just drives right through. The metal fence posts fly liked match sticks. We bounce around wildly like kids in the back of a school bus. I crack a little smile. I hear handgun fire coming at us. There is a security guard station a couple of hundred metres from us. An airport security guard fires many shots at us from his handgun. The MINI guns on the Scorpions open fire on him and quickly there are no more rounds coming at us. Smoke and dust are all that is left where a man once stood.

The one Scorpion helicopter drops in to pick up our three guys from the roof top just before they are over run by the enemy. The other Scorpion helicopter continues to fire at the swarm of men trying to over run our guys. I look back to see the Scorpion taking off from the roof top. The AWACS Commander directs the Scorpions to meet near the ground teams at the extractions point. I see the Scorpion with my guys fly low over us as if to stick their tongues out at us.

We are driving very fast now down the runway towards the Scorpions that are just landing. I hear another MINI gun open up. I can't see who is firing or what they are firing at, only that there is a lot of smoke and noise. We pass the control tower and are flying by some hangers. The teams are just coming into view now. There is no visible daylight yet and everything is glowing green from my night vision gear. I turn back to look at the Colonel and he does not look good. Johns is still tending to him. He is squeezing in the last bag of intravenous solution in a hope to save the man's life. If I had a choice to have anyone looking after me if I was shot, it would be Johns. He would bust a gut to save a life. The Colonel opens his eyes and looks right at me. I reach down pat him on the shoulder. "We're almost there Colonel. Hold on we'll have you on the Scorpion in just a minute," I say calmly to the man. He gives me a little smile and closes his eyes once again.

There is still continued MINI gun fire and the air is heavy with the acrid smell of gun smoke. We pass the first of the reserve forces and somehow I feel safe as we just crossed some imaginary line. We are inside the security perimeter. We drive to the nearest Scorpion and come to a screeching halt. We are met by a group of medics who quickly take over from Johns. I look at him and give him a big smile. The noise from the Scorpion is deafening. "You're the man I'd want working on me if I got shot," I yell at him. "I think I've done that," he reminds me. More than once he has had to fix me up. The Colonel is loaded onto the Scorpion and quickly it takes off. He is gone.

I look at Johns and he is covered in the Colonel's blood. His hands are stained red and he has a smear of blood on his cheek. He looks exhausted, haggard. He slings his medical bag back around on his back. Looks at his weapon and sees it too is covered in blood.

Sims and Calloway come running over to where Johns and I are standing. "AWACS command to Red leader, regroup and stand by for further instructions," he commands. Having heard the AWACS Commander, Johns looks at me with some curiosity. I shrug my shoulders and kneel down. I take a long drink from my camel back. I see others do the same. Johns hands me a power bar. I guess he figures we are going to need it. I eat it quickly and take another big drink. Scorpions continue to land and take off with teams of men.

"AWACS command to Red leader," he asks for my attention. "Red leader send AWACS command," I ask for more information. "AWACS command, the two American teams, Orange and White are cut off from the main group. Please see the map on your HUD, I am sending now," he asks. Immediately a map pops up on my HUD and I see two harden positions to my west that are occupied by the enemy. There seems to be some kind of concrete bunkers that have multiple machine guns. These bunkers are on the edge of the airport and face the main highway coming into the airport. The Americans can't cross the road from their position or come across the air field. Behind them are buildings that are too far to run to in the open. The MINI guns have no effect on the concrete. I suspect that the two bunkers that are about
three hundred metres from each other are joined by a tunnel. I can see on my HUD that the Americans are

pinned down but currently all OK. They are in a small ditch next to the main highway.

"AWACS command to Red leader, you need to take out the two bunkers so the Scorpions can land and extract all teams safely. There are Scorpions standing by for your extraction. Do you copy?" he asks. "Red leader, how did these two teams get there and why can't they make their way back the same way?" I ask. "AWACS command, I do not know, we were not online at that time," he states flatly. "Red leader, to Orange and White team leaders, how are your stealth suits?" I ask. "Orange leader, all of our suits on both teams are down. The rain has killed our batteries," he sounds frustrated.

I look down at my suit status and see that my batteries are also extremely low, too low to do this mission. Everyone else looks at their suit status. All of my guys shake their heads NO. "AWACS command to Red leader, we already anticipated this and there is a Scorpion en route to drop supplies to you now." As he finishes his sentence we see the Scorpion swoop in low towards us, the side door opens and two metal strong boxes are tossed unceremoniously out. The Scorpion never touches down. In ten seconds it is out of sight once more, as if it was never there.

"Red leader to AWACS command, we are going to need that Scorpion to continue the assault until we are in place," I ask. "AWACS command, understood Red leader. Scorpion will provide cover until you are in place," he confirms. We walk over to where the strong boxes are and open them. We start by taking off our used batteries and opening the packages of the new one and installing them. My batteries are on my back and I hand mine to Johns and he puts them in for me, I do the same for him. Sims and Calloway's batteries are on their belts and they replace their own. I grab a bottle of water and drink it all quickly. Everyone does the same. I reach up and turn my mic off, everyone follows suit. I grab four grenades, two flash bangs and two fragmentation grenades.

"So what's the plan boss?" Sims asks me. "Well, we're going to go stealth. Walk right up to the front and stick our fuckin' heads in and shoot them. Get the fucking Americans safely out. Pack our shit up, and go the fuck home," I say with a grin. "It's been a long fucking night," Calloway says. Everyone nods their heads in agreement. "Why and the fuck do we always have to pick up the pieces when shit goes horribly, horribly wrong?" Sims ask. "'Cause we're the only ones who can," I look at him and smile. If the truth be known, that is a fact. We are the best. We may not say it, but we are.

It's early morning and the sun peaks through the dark clouds. I turn my mic back on. "Red leader to AWACS command, can you give us a weather report?" I ask. "AWACS command, there are showers moving in your direction. You have about twenty minutes until they arrive. We are moving AWACS command to a lower altitude so not to be cut out if there are thunderstorms," he states. "Red leader out," I end the conversation.

I reach up and turn my mic back off. "Let's take the first one. Go in and see if there is a connecting tunnel. If there is a tunnel we'll follow it and see what we get" I say confidently. "I'll take the point and Calloway takes the rear," Johns suggests. I nod my head in agreement. "Let's keep our shit tight and get this done," I nod.
Everyone agrees. "Were going to go stealth and walk right up to the gun opening and take them. Johns and I will go around to the left you two go right," I command. They all give me a thumb up. I reach up and turn my mic back on and everyone does the same. "Red leader to AWACS

command, we are going stealthy. Our strobes are on," I inform him. "AWACS command, copy that Red leader we have your strobes. You are a go," he finishes. We all just disappear. I can see my guys in my HUD and we begin to quickly work our way over to the first enemy hardened position. Johns leads followed by myself, Sims and then Calloway covers the rear. We move at a quick jog over to the first objective. As we get near I sling my rifle and pull out my handgun.

We clear a long open area and make it to a ditch about two hundred metres from the first bunker. The ditch is full of rain water from the night's thunderstorm but we jump it and move on. The sun is still low in the sky and the air is still cool and damp. The grass is soaking wet. We are about one hundred metres from the bunkers. "Red leader to Red team split up now," I order. Johns and I move to the left and Sims and Calloway go to the right. We slow

down as we approach the sides of the bunker.

"Red one to AWACS Command, stop the Scorpions from firing now," immediately they stop firing. The SHIT suits are great at camouflage, but don't do anything for noise

reduction. We are right up to the sides by the opening.
"Red leader, Johns and Sims on my mark are you ready," I
whisper. "Red two ready," says Johns. "Red three ready,"
says Sims. I can hear shuffling around and some low
talking coming from inside the bunker It sounds like three
voices. "Red leader to Red team, three, two, one,
MARK," I finish. I look at my HUD. I see Johns and
Sims react, perfectly in sync, perfectly silent. I don't hear
the shots, but I do hear the sound of bodies hitting the
floor like bags of wet cement. Johns climbs in the front of
the bunker followed by Sims. "Red two to Red leader, we
are clear."

"There are two openings, each about five feet wide and
two feet high. There is what appears to be a tunnel,"
Johns says coolly. "Red leader to AWACS command, we
are going to take the tunnel. Be advised there is a lot of
concrete here we may lose the signal," I inform him.
"AWACS command we will monitor Red leader," he
replies. I figure if it starts to rain again our stealth won't
be interrupted if we are inside the tunnel. I jump up and
grab the concrete wall and pull myself into the dark
bunker. My HUD automatically changes to night vision
and again everything is an eerie green colour. I see four

dead men on the floor all have a single bullet wound to the head. There is a communications centre that is buzzing with traffic. I don't understand anything that is being said, but it sounds like they are in a hurry. I move over towards the tunnel and take a couple of steps in. "Red leader to AWACS command, how is our signal?" I ask. "AWACS command we have adjusted. Your signal is fine. There are three men in a room down the tunnel on the left hand side, about twenty metres," he informs us. I look at my guys. They all nod.

Johns once again takes the point position. He has his handgun raised and he looks down the sights. The tunnel is mostly unlit except for a couple of dim yellowy wall mounted lights. The air is damp and feels heavy to breathe. We continue down the tunnel. I can hear some muffled speaking. We get nearer. My heart beats hard in my chest. I look at my HUD. There are seven men in the room. Four appear to be at a table and three others scattered around the room. "AWACS command to Red leader, three men approaching from your front and to the right, hallway," he says quickly. Johns kneels down. I move past the door quickly. The door to the room is open only slightly. I hear footsteps coming ever closer. The men begin to yell as they move down the hall towards us. I can't see them yet. There they are now. They are on my HUD. I hear the door behind me smash open and see Johns, Sims and Calloway burst into the room on my HUD. The yelling from the three men to my front grows panicked. Ten metres, they come even closer. My handgun is raised and I lean against the wall to steady myself. I glance at my HUD. My guys have all joined me. The men are calling frantically now, to their dead comrades. I think to myself, "the jig is up, they know we are here". They round the corner and we all fire simultaneously. There are multiple shots fired and the three men drop dead at my feet. One pins me against the wall and I kick myself free. "Fuck that was close!" I say. "Red leader to Red team, are we clear? Check!" I ask.

The men at my feet are all dead. Johns and Sims go back to make sure all of the others are dead. They nod to assure me. "Fuck it doesn't get any closer that that," Sims says. "AWACS command to Red leader, get out of there now! There are multiple troops making their way towards you now!" he warns. We all turn and run back towards the bunker opening. I quickly sling my rifle and jump up and clear. Someone hits me on the way out. I roll clear.

There is a lot of yelling coming from the men inside the bunker. "Grenades!" I yell at my team. I grab a grenade and throw it inside, the others must have all done the same. The explosion is terrific. The smoke and shrapnel fly from the bunker opening. My head shudders from the force of the explosion. I shake my head to try and clear the cobwebs. "Holy fuck, I think it's clear," says Calloway.

All this is happening while the MINI gun on the Scorpion has been firing at the other bunker. "Red leader to AWACS command, can you get the MINI gun to lighten up on the other bunker and concentrate his fire on this bunker. Also let the Americans know we have cleared the first bunker and are on the way to the second?" I say. There is a lot of radio chatter. I hear Scorpion pilots talking to deck hand back on the aircraft carrier for directions as to where to land. I hear the ground forces who have already been extracted joking to each other, just a lot of random noise and we are still trying to win a battle down here. "Red leader to AWACS command can you clear some of this radio traffic? We need a clear channel, " I ask. "AWACS command, copy that Red leader. All radio traffic clear this channel immediately, for ground troop use!" he commands. The radio goes silent.

I am sprinting over to the other bunker. I feel a drop of rain and my pace quickens. My guys struggle to keep up to me, but they do. "What's the plan this time boss?" Sims asks. "Nothing fancy, throw grenades and run like hell," I struggle to say as I run. We circle around from the back. I grab a grenade and pull the pin. "Red leader to Red team, grab a grenade. Follow up with rifle rounds," I say calmly. "On my mark. Three, two, one, MARK!" I yell as I throw my grenade and duck back around the corner. The explosion is huge. When a lot of explosives are put into a small space the resulting explosion is devastating. My ears ring. My brain sloshes around like jelly in a bowl. My eyesight goes blurry. I fall to the ground with a thud. Everything goes black. I am in a haze. Then I hear rifle fire and realize I am in a battle. I grab my rifle and turn back towards the fight to find it already over. I am still dazed. I stumble. " AWACS command to Red leader are you alright? Your vital signs are going crazy," he asks. I can't answer. Everything is a fog. I feel my shoulder shaking. "Zeke you OK?" a voice asks. I try to clear my eyes, but I don't see anyone because we are still in stealth. My mind starts to clear. I look at my HUD. I see Johns in front of me. The world comes a little clearer every second. "Yeah I'm good," I say. But really I'm not. "Red two, to AWACs command, Red leader just got his bell rung a little is all. He is coming around now," Johns says.

I stand up a little straighter and start to move. "Red leader, I'm Ok, now," I say as my mind starts to clear. "Red leader to AWACS command get those Scorpions in here now. Orange leader and White leader the bunkers are clear make your way over here for extraction," I command. I can already hear the Scorpions coming. We move over towards a clear piece of road. I see the Americans running towards us. I can hear gunfire in the

distance coming in our direction.

Four Scorpions flying low scream in towards us. One provides cover fire from its MINI gun and the other three land to pick us up. My heart pounds in my chest. I take a running leap towards the one nearest us and I can see my other three guys jump in behind me. As soon as we are in, the guns open up.

"Orange leader to Red team, thanks. We owe you one," he thanks us. "Red leader to Orange leader, anytime," I say. "White leader to Red leader, you got one hell of a team there. I'm glad you bastards are on our side. Thanks," he finishes.

I turn my stealth off, so does everyone else. "Holy fuck, do I look as tired as you fucks?" I ask. "No, you just look older," Sims says. We all laugh. I look at everyone individually and I smile. I realize these guys would do anything for me and I would do anything for them. This is as close to having a second family as is possible.

I look down at my hands. My gloves are dirty and worn. I take my helmet off and see world with my own eyes for the first time since leaving the sub. The Scorpion hums quietly against my back. We head out over the ocean towards the aircraft carrier. Everyone sits quietly looking very exhausted. I close my eyes and think of my wife and kids for the first time in awhile. I wonder where they are and what they are doing. I hope that by this time tomorrow I will be with them again. I miss my wife's kiss, holding the little hands of my kids, the way they laugh.

Rod Bergeron   177

Twenty minutes passes like a second and we are landing on the carrier. There are hundreds of people on the deck to welcome us, they all cheer and clap and pat us on the back. I am overwhelmed and a little shocked. I look at my guys and we all smile and have a nervous laugh together. I think this is the first time we have ever been publicly noticed. Usually there is no fanfare, no warm greetings, seldom even a thank you. This was completely different.

After about ten minutes of this we made our way below deck. We were lead down to the staging area where we started to shower and change. We are met by a Major just inside the door. "I am Major Brown. Guys, great job out there today. I wanted to tell you before you heard it second hand, the Colonel didn't make it," he says quietly. He pats me on the shoulder and walks off. I am stunned.

I walked over to where my bag was and pick it up and head over to a group of benches. Tears weld up in my eyes. I sit down on the bench. I set my helmet down and unlaced my boots. I kick them off into the corner. I look in my bag and find my running shoes. I take my vest off

Rod Bergeron

and started to pull my SHIT suit off and I realize I am covered in blood, the Colonel's blood. Tears race down my cheeks. A giant sadness over takes me and I struggle for some control. I have none. I shake and cry openly.

I hear others crying. I stand and turn the corner to see Johns with his head in his hands and crying uncontrollably. He is inconsolable. I sit down beside him and put my arm around his shoulder. He cries on me and puts his hand on my back. He looks me in the eye with tears rolling down his face and says, "I don't think I can do this anymore".

www.ingramcontent.com/pod-product-compliance
Lightning Source LLC
Chambersburg PA
CBHW051516170626
46811CB00002B/851